HOOP CITY

LOS ANGELES

SAM MOUSSAVI

EPIC
Press

Los Angeles
Hoop City: Book #1

Written by Sam Moussavi

Copyright © 2016 by Abdo Consulting Group, Inc.

Published by EPIC Press™
PO Box 398166
Minneapolis, MN 55439

Cover design by Nicole Ramsay
Images for cover art obtained from Shutterstock.com
Edited by Lisa Owens

LIBRARY OF CONGRESS CATALOGING-IN-PUBLICATION DATA

Moussavi, Sam.
Los Angeles / Sam Moussavi.
p. cm. -- (Hoop city)
Summary: Paul is the top high school basketball player coming out
of Los Angeles. Will the pressure of leading his team through his
senior season and choosing a college be enough to break Paul?
ISBN 978-1-68076-046-0 (hardcover)
1. Basketball—Fiction. 2. High schools—Fiction. 3. Inner cities—Fiction.
4. Teamwork—Fiction. 5. Young adult fiction. I. Title.
[Fic]—dc23
2015903976

EPIC
Press

EPICPRESS.COM

To Marina, with a white butterfly fluttering just above her shoulder

ONE

That's the thing about the game. Through all the smiles and pats on the back, through all the buzzer beaters and tough losses, you're the one who steps on that floor. You're the one who has to carry it.

———

"What are you thinking about, Paul," Coach DeStefano said, "in terms of colleges?"

"I'm still weighing everything, Coach," I said. "There's still time."

"Not so much," he said.

The excitement of the new season was always tempered with an anxiousness. It was always that way for me, no matter how good I was, no matter what my stature was on the team, since I was a little kid.

"Go to class," he said. "We'll talk after school."

I got up and headed for the door.

"Oh, and Paul," he said, with eyes looking down at a sheet of paper in his hands, "I want you to know that you can discuss anything with me, college or otherwise."

"I know, Coach."

There was always pressure in my life. On the court. In my neighborhood. Life was pressure. And it didn't help that I didn't have my parents to help me deal with any of it. I lost them when I was just a kid. My grandmother kept me off the streets. Her love was genuine. But she couldn't help with the pressure. That was on me.

I went to first period after meeting with Coach. It was twelfth grade English. I liked starting the day with words instead of numbers. My mind needed to get warmed up before dealing with numbers. It was like stretching before practice or a game. You couldn't just step out there on the floor and run at full speed. You needed to warm up first.

"Who wants to share their opinion on the beginning of the book?" Ms. Walker asked.

No one raised a hand. Typical. No one spoke up. That is, no one acknowledged the teacher's question, instead they just continued with their own conversations.

"Paul?" she said.

The room went quiet. Ms. Walker pushed me even though I played ball. I liked that. Plus, I thought that the books were interesting.

"What do you think about the beginning?" she insisted.

I could feel all of the eyes in the room on me. I was used to it. It didn't make me feel uncomfortable.

Just like on the court. Block out the crowd. They're not even there. It's just you, the man in front of you, and the hoop.

"I think the first chapter is a dream," I said. "And I think the narrator is trying to wrap his head around the fact that the dream is not going to end well."

"Interesting," Ms. Walker said, with a nod. "But how can one interpret a dream if they're in the midst of it? I mean, don't you have to be awake to remember a dream?"

Now I was silent. I had to think on that a little.

Ms. Walker smiled in my direction and she continued trying to teach the class. I appreciated her efforts, although I'm not sure anyone else in the class did.

"Psst! Paul!" someone whispered behind me.

I turned around. It was Devin. He was one of those kids who hung around the basketball team, but didn't play. He got along with mostly everyone on the team. I kept my distance from him though.

I couldn't read him. Couldn't tell if he wanted anything from me.

"Did you decide?" he whispered.

"Nah," I said and turned back around.

"Everyone's saying Southern California," he said to my back.

I ignored him, staying focused on the task at hand.

TWO

I was excited for my last season at Inglewood High. I was optimistic that this would be a good year. Not only for me but the whole team. And I hoped to stay healthy, both physically and mentally.

The first practice was always fun. Even though the team worked out together all summer and fall, that opening practice always had a little extra something. I was in perfect health, too. No sprained fingers. No turned ankles—yet. There were no lingering injuries from the season before. There's nothing worse than trying to play when you're not at full strength. That happened to me early on, during sophomore year, when I landed awkwardly on my tailbone going after a wild alley-oop attempt. I couldn't walk right the whole rest of the season. But I never missed a game. Coach DeStefano said that he hadn't seen a player as tough as me at Inglewood High since Paul Pierce walked through the halls. That was saying something in itself. Paul Pierce aside, my school had plenty of tough players from South Central. Players who made it all the way to the pros and everywhere in between. South Central was known for its toughness. And I was glad to be a part of that, in my own little way.

Coach wasn't in his office and I didn't wait around. I got my ankles taped by Wendy, our trainer, and I hit the court to warm up. No one else was out there yet. The silence suited me just fine. I liked getting a look at the gym before it was filled with squeaks and hollers. I could picture in my head what I wanted to get accomplished for that practice, for the season. I ran through my drills to warm up, the same ones that I used from age seven, when I first picked up a basketball. When my dad first put it in my hands, that is.

I had already broken a sweat and practice wouldn't start for another fifteen minutes. Finally, the others joined me. Terrell was first, my point guard and teammate since sophomore year, when we were the only non-upperclassmen on the team. He was also highly recruited and had already made the choice to stay home and go to UCLA. He's always urged me to do the same, even before he signed. That made me wonder if UCLA had cut a deal with him. That if he got me to sign with them, they would then give him a full ride. I was relieved when he signed with UCLA. I didn't want anyone making any deals behind my back.

The rest of the team started coming out in pairs. That was how it went since the middle of junior year. Me first. Then Terrell. Then the rest of the squad.

The whole team lined up to stretch with Terrell and me at the front.

"You early, son," Terrell said.

"Yeah, I had a meeting with Coach," I said, "but he was out."

"You decide?"

"Nah."

"Just come to UCLA," he said. "You get to stay home. Plus the bitches are fly."

I shook my head. "I gotta think about it some more."

"You better hurry up, son. Ain't too much more time to sign."

Terrell always called me *son* and I wasn't really sure why. It didn't make much sense because I was a way better player than him. No one would say otherwise. Also, I was older than him by a few months and taller than him by at least five inches. It was a friendly thing though and I didn't fuss about it. I didn't get the sense that he was trying to get one over on me by calling me *son*.

"There's time," I said. "There's always time."

I knew exactly how much time I had. And I planned on using every bit of it.

"Okay, let's go! Let's go!" Coach yelled, as he walked onto the floor with the assistants. "Circle up!"

We gathered around Coach.

"I want to welcome you all to the first practice of the year. We all have high hopes for the season and we want to end it the right way. We want it to end up at ARCO with us holding the trophy."

We were all silent. The team was an experienced one: six seniors, five juniors, and one sophomore. We knew when Coach wanted us to listen and we also knew when he wanted our input. There were talks and then there were discussions. Coach talked. We discussed. This was the first talk of the year. There was nothing to discuss. We all wanted to make it to ARCO Arena in March. That was the goal every year at Inglewood High. ARCO Arena was up in Sacramento and it was where the Kings played their home games. But it also served as the annual site for the California high school basketball championships. North versus south. Even though the name of the arena had changed from ARCO to Sleep Train Arena, we still called it "ARCO." It would always be ARCO. Sleep Train didn't have the right ring to it.

"Last year we made it to the Forum," Coach said.

The Inglewood Forum was where the City Championship is held. One step shy of ARCO.

"That was fine for last year," Coach continued. "But not this year. This year is our year. We're going up north this year. Believe it and you'll achieve it."

Coach scanned the group, looking into everyone's eyes until he focused on mine. He kept his eyes there and I looked right back at him.

"Okay, let's start with layups," Coach said.

———

I loved practice. Most players hated it. It bored them. But not me. I loved getting better. I loved working on my weaknesses. And most importantly, I found that practicing hard made the games easy for me.

We started with defense. That's the way it was with Coach. He didn't care about offense. He used to say to us that if we relied solely on our offense, that it would let us down when we needed it most.

You could tell that a team was working on defense from simply listening to sounds coming from the gym. No laughs. No shit talking. You wouldn't even hear a ball bouncing. Rubber soles squeaking on the hardwood were the only sounds you'd hear. And as soon as you thought it was over and that a break was coming, Coach would add five more minutes of stance work.

"Terrell!" Coach yelled, after blowing his whistle. "Get down in a proper stance! You're not at UCLA yet!"

Repetition. You had to learn to live in a defensive stance. You had to learn to love it. Embrace the burn, is what Coach called it.

Coach hired a professional trainer to prepare me for senior year. The trainer put me through two-a-day workouts this summer with the first one starting at seven a.m. Every workout that summer, before we ever picked up a basketball, there was defensive stance work. I took pride in my stance. No one was going to blow by me during senior year.

"Paul! Hell of a stance!" Coach yelled. The veins at the side of his head were bulging like a maniac's would. This was only twenty minutes into the first practice of the year.

"Do the rest of you see Paul? If our best player commits to defense like this then where are you? Just where are you?" Coach screamed.

After ten more minutes of that, Coach finally gave us a break. Everyone complained about the burn. Even Terrell. But not me. My legs were fine and strong.

"Yo, I'm dunkin' on you, son," Terrell said, before taking a sip of water. "First chance I get."

"Please," I said, without taking one sip. "I'm throwin' that shit back in your face if you try."

"We'll see," he said.

Coach gathered us up again. We all knew what time it was.

"Okay," he said. "Paul on one side. Terrell on the other."

Coach blew his whistle.

"Put twenty up there!" he yelled.

The scoreboard lit up with twenty minutes.

"Deonte, Al, Clifton, Jared—you're with Terrell. Paul, you got these four," Coach said, pointing to the four players I'd have on my side.

And with that, the first and only basketball was brought out for practice. I didn't care that Coach put all the seniors on Terrell's side. I wanted the responsibility. Besides, they weren't gonna be able to hold me. Not after the work I'd put in during the summer. Not after looking myself in the mirror and admitting there were holes in my game.

The ball went up and we won the tip. I handled

the ball for my squad even though the two spot was my natural position. That was one of my goals in the summer: to make the unnatural natural.

Terrell didn't guard me at the start of the scrimmage even though he usually did. I think he noticed the ten pounds of muscle I'd put on during the summer. And he also knew that my post-up game had improved from the year before and that I would have taken his little ass down low all day. Terrell was cat quick and deceptively strong, more threatening as a weak side defender than a primary one. My bigger concern for the scrimmage was Terrell knifing in for the steal when I had my back to him.

Deonte stepped up to guard me for the other side. He was my height—six foot five—and long. Defense was his thing and he was slated to be our defensive stopper. I had to show Coach that my work during the summer had paid off. Deonte was a good first test.

On my side's first three possessions, we scored. I assisted two of the buckets—they were both corner

three-pointers after I broke Deonte down easily
and got into the paint. The third score came from
me. They trapped me up top to get the ball out
of my hands and when I passed out of the double
team, their whole defense was scrambled. Terrell
ended up on me and I sprinted down into the
paint to grab an offensive rebound from a missed
corner three. I slammed the ball through the hoop
with two hands, glaring down at Terrell just for
effect.

He threw a forearm into my side and I laughed
it off.

"Damn," Deonte said, through strained breath-
ing as we ran down to the other end of the court.
"You ain't tired?"

I didn't say anything.

We led the scrimmage by twelve after ten
minutes. I wanted to hit the paint so I gave up
the ball-handling duties to a sophomore named
Malik. I scored on two straight possessions after
the switch. The first bucket came off a six-foot

fall-away. The second one came off a drop step, where I got Deonte in the air with a pump-fake, and then ducked under the help defense with a lefty lay-in.

On my third possession in the post, they came with an aggressive double team. Terrell surprised me, digging down hard for the trap, and deflected my pass. They stole the ball and got a dunk on the other end. I shook my head in disgust.

"You was getting a little too comfortable down there, son," Terrell said with another playful forearm to my side.

I knew the double teams would come. It's just that I didn't always anticipate where they would come from. Basketball is humbling like that. Just when you think you got it figured out, something surprises you and keeps you on your toes.

A few possessions later, they tried the exact same double team. When Terrell came down, I spun baseline, split two defenders, and dropped a bounce pass for Tommy, our six-foot-nine backup center. He laid the ball in and we went back up by double digits.

At the end of the first twenty minutes, my side was up forty-two to thirty. I had twelve points, eight rebounds, five assists, three steals, and a block. But that turnover out of the double team kept eating at me. I stood off to the side while the rest of the team drank water and toweled off. I had barely broken a sweat.

"You can't always get what you want," Coach said.

"I saw the double," I said. "It was just a little late."

"It's a little different down there, huh? The angles."

"Yeah. I'll get it," I said.

"I know you will."

"Tommy looks good. He's in shape."

"He looks good because he's playing with you."

"We're going another twenty, right?" I asked, finally wiping some sweat that pooled on my forehead.

Coach nodded and blew his whistle again. He made a few changes to both of the sides, but Terrell and I were still on opposite teams.

"Stop by the office after you shower," he said. "Things were hectic today."

"Okay, Coach."

The second half of the scrimmage started much like the first one. I handled the ball and assisted my teammates for easy scores. Coach put another strong defender on me and I treated him just like Deonte. I beat him with speed when he got too close and when he tried to get physical with me, I shrugged him off with head fakes and crossovers.

After the fifth possession or so where I assisted on a bucket, they switched up their strategy on me. My defender sagged off and two of the other defenders stayed glued to the corner shooters while the remaining two defenders roamed free to help with me. During my first three years on the team, my jumper was inconsistent. But my work over the summer—taking one dribble and pulling up, five hundred shots in the morning and five hundred in the evening—changed all of that for senior year.

It was time to unleash this new part of my game in the scrimmage. The defender sagged back again, almost daring me to shoot.

I took a dribble, got in rhythm, and knocked it down.

Next time we had the ball, I had it on the left elbow in triple threat position. I scanned the floor. There was no room to drive because they packed the lane. My man gave me space, once again daring me to shoot. One dribble. Elevate. Splash.

It was an amazing feeling. In my early years as a player, I was able to control the game physically. I could run faster and jump higher than all of the other players on the floor. And at six foot five, there were few people who could match up with me. But this was different. I could control the game mentally now. And that made me dangerous.

The buzzer sounded and the scrimmage was over. I looked up to the clock and read the triple zeros, realizing that I had played the entire scrimmage. I wasn't tired at all though.

Coach walked over to me, gave me a pat on the shoulder.

"I guess this means that you'll never want to come out of the games this season?"

I wiped a little more sweat off my forehead.

"The jumper feel good?"

"Real good."

"It looks good," he said.

Coach whistled. "Everybody gather up!"

The rest of the team circled around and Coach paced a bit before speaking.

"Just want to say I appreciate the effort I saw out there today. And I want to thank you all for the work you put in this summer. On your games. And on your bodies."

I looked around the circle and saw intensity in everyone's eyes. No one blinked. It was quiet in our little circle.

"There aren't gonna be too many teams that

can run with us for forty minutes," Coach said as he shook his head.

He paused before taking a step towards me. He motioned for me to join him in the middle of the circle.

"I know I usually name our captain before the first game of the season," he said. "But I'm ready now."

The whole team looked at me.

"Paul."

The guys clapped and whooped and hollered.

"Break us down, Paul," Coach said.

The circle got tighter and everyone put a hand in the center. All the guys looked at me as if they were waiting for me to take them somewhere. This was my first time ever being team captain. My on-court game spoke for itself. Now it was time to be a leader off the court and in the locker room.

I made sure that my voice was loud and clear.

"One! Two! Three!" I yelled.

"ARCO!" the rest of the guys yelled.

"Alright, hit the showers!" Coach said. "Go home and get that homework done! Don't be hanging out late and be aware of your surroundings!"

The guys went to the locker room and it was just me and Coach once again.

"This is your team," he said.

"I'm ready to do whatever you ask of me, Coach."

"Come to my office in fifteen minutes."

I nodded and headed towards the locker room.

———

All the newspapers said that we lost the City Championship at The Forum the year before because the other team took the ball out of Terrell's hands, forcing me to handle the ball. I had three turnovers late in the fourth quarter that led to seven points. The papers said that I was a finisher. And that's about it. They said I couldn't create for others. Make my teammates better. They also said I couldn't shoot worth a lick.

The defensive tactic that Coach threw at me during the scrimmage was the same one that had given me fits the year before in the City Championship game. Because of my driving ability and skill finishing at the rim, teams would no doubt copy this strategy and force me to shoot from the outside. With my jumper inconsistent, our offense would be compromised against good teams in big games. Our floor spacing would suffer and there would be no lanes to drive. That led to forcing my way through lanes that weren't there. That led to not trusting my handles enough to make plays. That led to not trusting my teammates. And that's when the turnovers occurred.

That was what ultimately led me to my summer of improvement. The added muscle, the new post-up game, the better handles. But most of all, the improved jump shot.

One dribble.

Pull up.

Splash.

Repeat.

No team was going to be able to beat us with that defensive strategy anymore. No team was going to beat us because I couldn't shoot.

ARCO would be our mantra for the rest of the year. In case we needed a reminder of our goal before a game or after a practice, ARCO was it. Getting there would be our mission. And it felt like it was my responsibility, mine alone, to get us there.

Make the unnatural natural.

THREE

I took a shower and then sat in front of my locker. The locker room had cleared out pretty quickly and I was the only one left. I enjoyed the silence for the few moments I had before meeting with Coach. I let my mind drift away from the college decision. I thought about my parents and sister even though there wasn't anything specific that caused me to think about them. That happened a lot with me. With a spare moment to get away from class and basketball, my mind went to them.

My life was hard. Not harder than most who lived in Watts. But hard enough. If it weren't for my grandmother, who knows where I would have been? That old cliché about the parent protecting their kid from the streets was definitely true for me. Except instead of a single mother, my story included a single grandmother.

I was lucky in the sense that I had both parents. And an older sister too. But that luck had run out early in my life. The three of them died in a car accident when I was five, and, just like that, the only family I had left was my grandmother. There were a couple of aunts and an uncle on my mom's side, but I never knew them because they stayed back in Mississippi when my mother left for college in LA. My dad was an only child and both of his parents were long dead before the accident.

It was just me and my grandmother. We shared a bond of loneliness. My grandfather—her husband—died shortly after he came home from the Vietnam War. I never got a chance to meet him. When I was small, Grandma told me that his heart just "gave out" one night. And when I asked what she meant by that she just stared back at me, the edges of her eyes wet with tears. The same thing has happened over the years when I would ask her about my parents. So, after awhile, I just stopped asking. Grandma didn't go back to Mississippi after the accident because she wanted to raise me in the house that my parents had bought. That was very important to her. Raising me in that house would be her way of honoring my parents' hard work.

Now the old cliché about the young black athlete being the first to go to college in their family was definitely not true for me. Both of my parents went to college. It's where they met: at USC. My mom was the first in her family to leave Mississippi, bringing my grandmother out west ten years later when her career got off the ground. My dad's family, on the other hand, was from Louisiana. He was like me, nowhere close to being the first to go to college in his family. Both of his parents went to Tulane University. Same for two of his uncles.

My way of branching out from the family tree came through basketball. But that didn't take anything away from the classroom for me. Through my parents, I gained a love of the classroom. It was really the only thing they were able to give to me in our short time together. That, and the house.

———

Coach was waiting in his office for me and it was already half-past eight. I hoped that the talk would be short, but you could never tell with him. He didn't take into consideration that I had homework to do along with taking care of my grandmother. To him, basketball was it for me and it would be a mistake if I didn't feel the same way.

"Sit down, Paul," he said.

I sat.

"Let's go through your list of colleges."

"Oh. I'm not ready to do that," I said. "I gotta prepare for something like that."

"Prepare what?" he said. "Give me your list."

I didn't say anything.

"You have a list, don't you?"

"Yes."

"So let me hear it."

"Coach, I gotta get home. Grandma is alone and—"

"Okay," he said, and I detected a bit of agitation on his face and in his voice. "But we have to talk about this. The deadline is coming up and you have to make the right decision. This is your future we're talking about. And I'm here to help."

"I know."

"Okay, get outta here," he said.

I got up to leave and Coach called my name. I looked up and he walked around to my side of the desk before saying, "You have a gift, Paul."

I nodded.

"You need a ride?"

"I'm gonna take the bus."

"Okay. Be careful out there."

"See you, Coach."

I left the office and the urgency of my decision carried a new weight. Coach was right. I had to make a choice. The deadline for seniors to commit was just a few weeks away and most players of my caliber had committed months, even years before.

Colleges started recruiting me between the summer of sophomore and junior year. That was when I had my growth spurt. But the process didn't get serious until the beginning of my junior year, when I cracked the starting lineup of the varsity team and began dominating on the court. It went smoothly at first; scouts came to my games and letters from interested schools flooded my mailbox. Then it came time for campus visits. And that's when my recruiting process started getting dirty. That dirt caused me to step away from the process and became the reason I had trouble making a decision on what school I'd attend. I decided to take my time and make a clean decision. I didn't want to be a part of the dirt.

———

The bus was late as usual and I was the only one waiting for it. It took two buses to get from school to my house and it always took a while to get home after practice because there were fewer buses circulating. I'd catch a ride with teammates if I could, but I didn't like getting a ride from Coach. Especially now. He'd no doubt bug me about my decision the whole ride home.

Terrell was already home. He started driving himself to and from school after he committed to UCLA. A man with ties to UCLA put a brand new Mercedes in Terrell's mom's name even though she didn't have a job or the money to pay the car note. Terrell didn't know anything about the man, just that he was a *friend* of UCLA. He told me that UCLA would arrange to do the same for me if I committed to them. I told Terrell that the bus suited me just fine. Coach knew about the car and the friends of UCLA that were hanging around Terrell and trying to hang around me. He knew about all of it, but chose not to acknowledge it. That was his way of rationalizing it. All of it.

The bus came and it was almost empty except for me and three older men sitting at the front. They looked tired, like they were just getting off work. Their eyes were the most tired things on their bodies. And right then was when the tired feeling hit me. My legs, which only one hour before were invincible, now felt like jelly.

I got off on Slauson and Normandie to wait for my second bus. It didn't take long and that was a relief. There were many nights where both of my buses were late and I didn't get home until way past nine o'clock. It was a small victory.

I started down Crenshaw and came up on Inglewood Park Cemetery. I stopped when I was about a hundred feet away from the front gate. Then I did what I always did when the cemetery came into sight. I crossed to the other side of the street. The cemetery was two blocks away from home. I could look out of my window and see the rows of marble sticking out of the green grass. My parents and sister were somewhere in there. I never walked near the cemetery, let alone in it. And my grandmother never took me there either. We shared that understanding. It reassured us to know that our people were right outside our window. But to go any closer than that was unnecessary. The window suited us just fine.

I continued down Crenshaw on the other opposite side of the cemetery.

My house was on Crenshaw and Florence. When I walked inside the door, it was eight forty-five. My grandmother was sitting in her old chair waiting up for me. She couldn't sleep unless she knew I was home safe.

The volume on the television was low. Just how she liked it.

She got up to hug me like she always did and after the embrace she smiled up at me. It was a familiar smile, one mixed with a little bit of sadness. She was a short, strong women. And even though she was old, she hadn't aged badly. There was still a sturdiness to her. My mother was an athlete just like me in her day and I often wondered which one of her parents she got that from. From the looks of old pictures of my grandfather, it seemed like the answer to that question was my grandmother.

"Those people been calling all day, Paul," she said.

"That right?" I said, with a smile.

"There's a list by the phone."

"Any food, Grandma?"

"In the oven," she said. "Nice and warm."

"Thanks, Grandma."

She sat back down and I went into the kitchen to eat. I ate in three minutes. I didn't even feel that hungry until I sat down to eat. Much like my delayed reaction to fatigue on the bus, hunger struck like an aggressive double team out of nowhere.

I took the list by the phone, folded it and put it in my pocket. I helped my grandmother to bed, kissed her on the forehead and turned off the light.

It was ten o'clock by the time I sat down at the desk in my room to finish my homework. My teammates couldn't understand why I cared about my classwork and I never tried explaining it to them. To them, I was just a ball player and that meant that classes and homework took a backseat. But I didn't look at it that way. If my parents were alive, they'd expect me to go to college—basketball or otherwise.

I finished my math and science that was left over from study hall and then I got into bed with the novel from English class. I thought about what Ms. Walker said about dreams earlier that day. I thought about the couple of mistakes I made during the scrimmage. And finally, I thought about my parents and my sister. I thought about everything but the decision until I fell asleep and traded my thoughts in for dreams.

FOUR

There was no shortage of girls at school who wanted to get with me. But I didn't know how to talk to them, because I didn't have a lot of experience. There were a couple of problems. First, I was always so busy with basketball that I just didn't have the time. And because of that, I never had a real girlfriend—ever.

The second problem stemmed from an incident that happened during junior year. After taking an official campus visit to an interested school, I decided that I was going to sign a letter of intent to play basketball at the school. The visit was the usual: tour of the campus and athletic facilities, meeting with the coach and some of the players on the team and going to a party at a frat house on campus. I was comfortable with the school and what it had to offer from academic and basketball standpoints. I felt comfortable committing to them.

Two days after I told Coach about my decision, he asked me to his office and said that he'd received a call from the athletic director of the college that I was planning to commit to. The AD told Coach that a girl from the frat party had accused me of rape and that she'd be pressing charges. The college pulled its scholarship offer and I was left out in the cold.

I didn't touch a single girl at that frat party, let alone rape one. There were girls throwing themselves at me and the rest of the players on the team. It creeped me out that these random girls would want to sleep with potential recruits. But I didn't accept. I didn't do anything wrong.

I remembered never feeling so low as I did when that rumor got out.

The only person on my side was Coach. When I told him what happened at the frat party, he told me not to worry and that it was just a rumor—that my accuser was offended by my not taking her up on her offer of free sex. Coach assured me that everything would be okay. He promised me that he would take care of it, and that I didn't have to talk to the cops.

About a week later, it was all taken care of. The accuser dropped her claim against me and there would be no investigation. I don't know what Coach did to resolve it and I didn't care. I had to start the recruiting process all over again. But so what? That was a small price to pay for being out from under that vicious rumor.

And after a little while, schools became interested in me again. I made the decision to not take another campus visit. I was going to take every moment I had to study the schools that were studying me. I was going to take my time with it. I wasn't going to let anyone pressure me. That approach went for girls, too.

There was this one girl, in my third period science class. Her name was Robin and she was just my type. Even though I didn't know what my type was. She had these tiny lips and when she smiled—which wasn't often—there was a little bit of sadness in there. Like there was something underneath, hidden. And from what I could tell, she didn't share her smile with many people. She would share it with me from time to time, though.

She was the only girl in school that I was comfortable talking with, or even being around. We were lab partners, that probably had something to do with it. I didn't know for sure, but what I did know was that when she was around, I didn't feel anxious or awkward. I could actually hold a conversation with her without feeling anything extra. It was just natural.

One day in science class, as the teacher talked about the frog we were about to dissect, I couldn't stop looking at Robin. She had these light eyes, the color of them was almost like caramel or something, and when she looked at me, I got knots in my stomach. The pressure of a basketball game never did that to me. Yet Robin's eyes did.

She caught me staring at her eyes and she gave me her little sad smile.

"What?" she said.

"Nothing," I said, fumbling around with my lab materials.

The door to the classroom opened and closed and a student gave a note to the teacher. She dropped her scalpel and took the note. She read it aloud: "Paul, go to the office. They need you."

The class *ooh*'ed.

Except Robin.

"You better get back to class and help me with this thing," Robin said as she tapped her pencil against the covered tray containing the dead frog.

"I'll be back," I said.

She flashed her eyes again and focused them right on mine. She also had this knowing smile, like I wasn't really going to come back and help her cut up that frog. Like whatever they needed me for in the office was way more important than what was going in class. And I thought how nice it would be to get lost in her eyes. I could look at her eyes all day and not get bored.

I left the classroom and walked through the empty halls. I walked past the main office and straight to the gym instead. I knew what a note from the office during class hours meant. It meant that Coach wanted to talk to me. Not the principal. I didn't understand why Coach kept sending notes through the main office. I couldn't get why he had to continue to lie.

I walked through the dark gym and into the empty locker room. On the way to Coach's office, there was a sign over a door that read: ACT AND PLAY LIKE A SENTINEL. Our team name was the Sentinels and it was tradition for the athletes at Inglewood High to tap that sign before they went out on the court or field. It was supposed to bring good luck for the season to the team. My teammates always tapped the sign for luck. But I never did. I didn't believe in luck and besides I didn't even know what a sentinel was until I looked it up—and if I didn't know, my teammates sure as hell didn't either. It seemed stupid to me to look to something like a sign to bring you good luck. And it seemed double stupid to not know what something meant and still hold it in respect.

I walked right under that sign like I always did and when I got to Coach's office, the door was open and he was at his desk looking over some papers.

"Paul," he said over his reading glasses. "Sit."

I took a seat and just sat there quiet.

"So?" he said.

"What?"

"What are you thinking?"

"About what?"

"Paul," he said, with emphasis.

"I'm still doing my homework, Coach," I said. "There's time."

"Yeah, but not much."

I didn't say anything.

He sighed.

"Paul," he said. "Do you need some help?"

"No, Coach," I said. "I appreciate what you're doing for me."

I paused.

"What you've done," I said. "But I think I need to take my time and make the right decision here."

"How do you know it'll be the right decision if you've never done it?" he said. "I've been doing this for fifteen years, Paul."

He pointed to the door.

"You know how many players have walked through that gym and into this office and sat in that seat you're sitting in to have this very conversation?"

"It'll be right because it'll feel right, Coach."

He sighed again, but this time tossed his glasses

onto the desk and rubbed the bridge of his nose. He got up from his desk and sat on the edge of it that was closest to me.

He pulled a sheet of paper out of his pocket. It was folded in fours. He handed it to me.

"I want you to take a hard look at those, Paul," he said.

I unfolded the sheet and there was a list of three schools on it.

I looked up at Coach. He didn't say anything.

I started to speak but Coach lifted his hand to cut me off.

"You better get back to class, Paul," he said. "Only fifteen minutes left before the bell."

I got up from the chair and headed towards the door. Before walking through it I turned around.

"Hey Coach," I said. "How come you pulled me out of class just to tell me this? Couldn't we have talked about this after school?"

He smiled and said, "Class is out, Paul." He pointed to his mantle, where a state championship plaque stood encased in plastic. "This is your salvation."

I left his office and walked back through the empty halls. The sheet of paper from Coach stayed in my palm until I got back to class. I slid it in my back pocket before going back into the classroom. I could feel the weight of it all the way back to my seat.

FIVE

R obin and I walked down the hall together after class. She was one of the few girls at school who didn't like sports and she made a point to tell me a few different times that she usually didn't like guys who played sports either. I was the exception to her rule about athletes. That rule made her attractive in my eyes, even more so than her eyes and smile.

"What was that all about?" she said, looking up to me as we walked.

"Some stuff with Coach," I said.

"He just pulls you out of class like that?"

"Yeah, when he needs me, I guess," I said.

She didn't say anything as we continued walking down the hallway towards the cafeteria and neither did I. People stared at us as we walked by, whispering and pointing fingers. I could tell that being seen around school with the star basketball player was uncomfortable for her. But she kept on walking with me nonetheless. The silence was uncomfortable for me, too, and usually that's where my interaction with females would die. But this time, for some reason, I used it as an opening.

"Robin," I said. "I was thinking . . . "

"Yeah," she said.

We stopped in front of the entrance to the cafeteria. Terrell was there talking to a couple other girls and I caught him eyeing me with Robin.

"I was thinking we could go to a movie some time," I said.

She smiled. It was the sweetest, saddest smile I had ever seen.

"Do you have time for that?" she said.

"Yeah," I said. "I'm free this Sunday. I know you don't like to come to the games. So we could go on Sunday."

"I'd like that, Paul," she said. "Let me put my number in your phone."

"I don't have a phone," I said.

"You don't have a phone," she said, with disbelief in her voice. "Why not?"

"I had one," I said. "But scouts kept calling and texting me, day and night. It got so bad that I had to keep changing numbers. But they kept getting the new numbers somehow. I decided that having a cell phone wasn't worth it. At least until I make my decision."

She nodded and dug in her bag for a pen and paper. She wrote her number down, folded the paper into fours and handed it to me.

"Call me anytime," she said.

I took the paper and slid it into my back pocket. It had a different weight than the other slip of paper that I had in my back pocket.

"I'll do that," I said.

She laughed a little. "See you around," she said.

"See you."

She went into the cafeteria.

And I knew what was coming next.

"What up, son," Terrell said. "You get them digits or what?"

"Yeah."

"Robin—yeah, she nice," he said. "It's about time."

"Yeah, whatever."

"What did Coach want with you?"

"How'd you know about that?" I said.

He smirked. "I know."

"He wanted to talk about—"

"You make up your mind yet?"

"I'm still thinking about it," I said.

"Damn, son. What's taking you so long?"

I didn't reply. On the court, I could shut Terrell up easy. But off it, he could be pushy if you kept responding to him. It was best to let him keep talking in the hope that he would tire himself out.

"You need to commit to UCLA," he said. "They keep asking me to help them recruit you."

I still didn't reply. I tried to walk past him and into the cafeteria but he grabbed me by the shoulder before I went inside.

"Just take a visit," he said. "There's still time."

"No more visits," I said with anger and volume in my voice. I glared at him as everyone around us in the hallway stared. You could hear a pin drop. I felt everyone's eye on me. But it wasn't a good feeling. Not like when I was on the court.

Terrell should have understood better than anyone that I was through with campus visits. Either he forgot or he underestimated me.

"My bad," he said. "I'm just looking out for you is all."

He put his hand out for a dap and I reluctantly did the same. We were the best players on the team and I wanted to make sure we had good chemistry.

Our approaches couldn't have been any more different, though.

"I'll see you at practice," I said.

He nodded and I walked into the cafeteria.

———

I got back to the locker room to get ready for practice before anyone else. That wasn't uncommon; I liked the quiet in there before the guys came in with their yapping. When I got to my locker, there was a newspaper wedged in between the lock. I knew what it was before even looking at it. It was the *LA Times* high school basketball preview. A reporter from the *Times* interviewed me for a profile three weeks back. He followed me for a day to my classes and workouts. He'd said he wanted to "get a day in the life of a blue-chip high school athlete." After the evening workout, I asked the reporter if he got anything interesting for the story. He just shrugged his shoulders. What he didn't do was follow me onto my two buses home that night. He didn't come to Watts when the sun went down, though he did ask me a question about how it feels to be so close to getting out. The reporter did make it to Watts a few days later though—albeit during the day. He came by to interview my grandmother, to get, in my own words, "the poor orphan angle." But she didn't say much, if anything at all. I laughed in the kitchen as the reporter "interviewed" my grandmother in her chair in the living room, trying his best to get her to talk, but failing miserably. At the end of it, the reporter asked me a question about the recruiting mess from my junior year and, on Coach's advice, I gave him the two most wonderful words in the English language as an answer: "No comment." He smiled and said I was ready for the NBA. I smiled back and asked him to leave the "No comment" out of the article—also Coach's advice. He said he would and then left my grandmother's house in Watts. And I guessed that he wouldn't set foot in

South Central again—at least until next season's preview edition. Where he'd be in some single mother's home, asking her what it feels like to have her son so close to leaving the only home he's ever known.

The article was boring. Like I thought it would be.

"They picked us to go thirty-and-O," a voice said over my shoulder.

I looked back and saw that it was Terrell.

"You saw it already?"

"Yeah. Who you think put it in your locker, son?"

"Who cares about this?" I said, as I threw the paper in the garbage can. Perfect swish.

"They say you're gonna lead us all the way to ARCO," he said, as he picked the paper out of the can. He read aloud from it: "The number one prospect in the greater LA area, Paul Stephenson, will lead his team to not only a sectional title, but a state one, too."

I didn't say anything, hoping that the rule of Terrell would kick in once again.

"Not much about me," he said.

"It doesn't mean anything," I said. "You got a full ride to UCLA. The rest of the team looks up to you. I know how important you are."

"It means something," he said.

"No one in this locker room cares about the article. The person who wrote it has never stepped on a basketball court."

Terrell didn't say anything right away. I was a little surprised and unsure of what to say next. I turned around to open my locker and get changed for practice.

"You with me, Paul?" he said.

I couldn't even remember the last time Terrell called me *Paul* and when he did, it put a smile on my face. I turned back around and the look on his face was serious. And it was strange because no matter what the situation, Terrell always had a smile on his face. It didn't matter if he was in the hallways or on the court, you could always locate Terrell by the smile. It was his way of keeping calm through a hard life, I supposed. I, on the other hand, played the game with no expression at all. My teammates used to talk shit during film sessions, calling me Stone Face. And if you caught me off the court I was known to have that same expression . . . of no expression.

"Yeah, I'm with you, T," I said. "I'm with you."

I put my fist out for a pound and he did the same. The smile didn't come back onto his face.

"See you out there," he said.

I nodded as I unbuttoned my shirt and turned back to my locker.

The season would be difficult no matter what. Every season was. Our goal of reaching the States in Sacramento would bring pressure day in and day out. I sighed deeply after I put my practice uniform on. It was a heavy sigh, made heavier by the folded sheet of paper in the back pocket of my jeans. The one from Coach. But I had to put it out of my mind, at least while I was at practice. I couldn't let my individual goals derail the team ones. I hoped that Terrell felt the same. He was a fellow senior and fantastic player in his own right. He could help ease that burden on me, if only just a bit. But after that exchange about the *Times* article, the weight on my shoulders seemed to multiply. I knew we would have no chance if the team became divided, if Terrell and I became divided.

SIX

Practice was an intense one. Terrell came at me as hard as he could and I returned the favor. His demeanor from the locker room lingered onto the court. He kept a serious tone, both on his face and in his body language. If that was his way of improving his play from the year before, it was fine by me. He was as focused as I had even seen him. The whole team really.

Terrell usually couldn't score on me if I locked him up defensively. My quick feet and long arms made it hard for him to create a shot. But he had added some stuff to his game over the summer, too. And it would only make us better as a team.

Coach matched us up against one another in the scrimmage and we went back and forth exchanging buckets. For every drive and lay-in that I had, he answered with a step-back jumper that just cleared my fingertips.

It's not that we were ignoring the rest of our teammates on the floor. It's just that we were both in the zone. And the number one rule when you are in the zone is to stay in the zone. And the only way to do that is to keep shooting. In practice it is harmless when a star player—or in this case, two—go back and forth, trying to stay in the zone. You can laugh off wild shots during practice. But in a game, you have to understand that being in the zone can't go on at the expense of teamwork. Having Terrell locked in like he was, able to join me in the zone, would make the game that much easier for me and the rest of the team. But once in the zone, would Terrell be willing to make the pass? That I didn't know yet. And our season probably hinged on it. Smart players know how to handle being in the zone. I thought of myself as a smart person and player. I wasn't sure about Terrell.

"Your step-back is on point," I said to Terrell, as we ran back down the floor.

The buzzer sounded and there was a break in the scrimmage. Terrell and I walked over to the bench with the rest of the team.

"Yeah," he said finally, before taking a sip of water.

"Just make sure in a game, when the defense cocks to you like that," I said. "That you swing the ball."

He took another sip of water and stared at me as he gulped it down.

"It'll come right back to you if you move it early," I said.

"Got you," he said, before running back onto the court.

When the scrimmage resumed, Terrell and I went right back at it. My question was answered with regard Terrell's handling of being in the zone.

Whereas I used my teammates after the break in the scrimmage, Terrell tried and tried to stay in the zone. He tried to split double teams that couldn't be split, forced deep jumpers that I contested aggressively, and the result was the disruption of his side's offensive flow. My side broke away and cruised to victory. He failed the first test. But it was only the second practice of the season. I decided to give him a pass because he wasn't used to being in the zone offensively. He could learn how to deal with it. I could help him, if he was willing. I went through the same exact thing the season before.

Practice ended and Coach gathered us up at center court.

"Great job out there guys," he said, before pausing to think.

The rest of the guys looked on at him, waiting for him to speak. Terrell's eyes were somewhere else. He knew what was coming.

"Terrell, if that were in a game, I would have to pull you out," Coach said.

"Coach—" Terrell said.

"I don't want to hear anything from you," he said, raising his voice slightly. "You need to listen. That's not your game. I know you were feeling good out there, going back and forth with Paul, but that's not your role."

That was Coach's way. He wasn't afraid to go after a player in front of the team, even a star player. I respected that about him.

"You gotta be better than that," Coach continued.

I walked over next to Terrell and put an arm on his shoulder. I didn't want him to think he was alone in this.

Coach gave me a quick look and I nodded to him. He drew in a deep breath and stopped talking.

"I'm done," he said. "Let's break the huddle and hit the showers."

I led the huddle and we broke on "ARCO!" The guys took off for the locker room, but Terrell and I stayed behind. Terrell walked away from Coach and I and went down to the other end of the floor to cool off. He was frustrated and annoyed after being called out in front of the team. I could see it in his eyes and his body. His shoulders shrunk and he looked small and that was saying something because he was already small. But I wanted to know the source of his frustration.

Coach took a couple of steps towards where Terrell was.

"Let me get this, Coach," I said, cutting over in his path.

"I need to—" he said.

"I'll handle it," I said. "It's my job."

Coach smiled, patted me on the shoulder, and walked out of the gym. I waited until he was gone and it was just Terrell and me.

I walked over to the far end of the gym and Terrell's posture was still tense. He had his back to me.

"Yo, T," I said. "You want to talk on it?"

He didn't say anything, but at least he turned

around. His eyes looked like they were about to release some tears, but they didn't.

"Coach can be a little a harsh. He only did that to make you a better player."

"Fuck him!" Terrell shouted. The sound of his voice echoed in the empty gym.

"Don't take it personally," I said.

He didn't say anything.

"I know you worked on your offense this summer," I said. "I can see it out there."

"Yeah?"

"Hell yeah," I said.

He took a deep breath, relaxed his shoulders a little.

"Them niggas need to know, Coach too, that I can take over when you come out of the game," he said. "Or if you're having an off night."

I cracked a smile.

"You know I don't come out of the game," I said. "And you damn sure know that there won't be any off nights for me this year."

He shook his head and a smile finally came back onto his face.

"The rest of the guys know that," I said. "There's nothing for you to prove. You got your full ride. You're a leader on this team."

"You're the leader," he said with a little sharpness in his voice. "Just like that newspaper man said."

"That reporter is trying to drive a wedge up in here," I said. "Sell more newspapers."

He nodded.

"I need you, T," I said. "This year more than ever."

He took a deep breath and gave me dap and a half-hug. "I got you, son," he said. "Us."

"Us," I said.

"You need a ride home?" he said. "It's late and shit."

"Nah," I said. "I'm good with the bus."

We started to walk towards the locker room and we didn't exchange any more words. I was glad to squash the situation. It was my job as captain to take care of these kinds of issues that popped up. I just hoped that there wouldn't be too many more of them.

We walked into the locker room and most of the guys had already showered and changed. There were a few—the lazy ones—who took their time, listening to music and cracking jokes.

When I walked over to my locker, Terrell followed me.

"Paul," he said.

I looked at him.

He looked around the locker room and waited to speak. Even though there were only a few of us left, he hesitated.

"Yo, T," I said. "It's late and I really don't wanna hear about UCLA right—"

"Nah, not that," he said. "It's Coach."

"Coach?"

"Yeah, watch out for him."

"Watch out for what?"

"He foul."

"What do you mean?"

He looked around again.

"He'll fuck with your scholarship," he said, almost at a whisper.

I thought about the sheet of paper with the list of schools in my back pocket.

"Real foul," he said.

Terrell walked over to his locker, most of the anger and frustration flushed out of his body after talking with me. All he needed to complete the cleansing was a cold shower. But he wasn't the only one who needed a refreshing burst of cold water. I took the list that Coach gave me earlier and held it in my hand. I needed to cool off, too. And I needed to get clean.

———

Only Terrell, Deonte, and I were left in the locker room. Deonte was changed up and getting ready to leave. I was almost ready. Terrell was still in the shower. He was in there for about twenty minutes.

Terrell walked back into the locker room and sat down in front of his locker.

Deonte walked over to my locker.

"Yo, Paul," he said. "You need to show me that cross that you been doing. You put it between your legs instead of crossing it over."

"Yeah, I'll show you," I said, while buttoning up my shirt. I had one eye on Terrell and the other on Deonte.

"Yeah, do that, Paul," Deonte said, as he gave me dap. "Do that."

Deonte left to go home and it was just Terrell and me once again. He took his time getting ready and who could blame him? He had a car and would be home in no time. Me on the other hand? I had two buses to catch.

Terrell looked over to me from his locker.

"Don't you have two buses to catch, nigga?" he said, tiredly.

"Yeah," I said, still working on the same button as when Deonte was still there.

Terrell could see through my stalling.

I walked over to his locker and sat down next to him.

"What did you mean about Coach out there?" I said.

He looked over my shoulder to the hallway leading to Coach's office. His light was still on.

"Meet me in the parking lot," he said. "We shouldn't talk in here."

I nodded and walked back over to my locker. I packed up my stuff, threw my jacket on, and left Terrell alone in the locker room.

—

I leaned against the brick wall near the doors that led to the back parking lot. The only car there was Terrell's Mercedes. It was cold out and late. Too cold and too late to be waiting for two buses. I'd be taking Terrell up on his offer to drive me home tonight.

The door shot open and Terrell came out, bundled up in a heavy coat and beanie. Since practice ended, we had switched places. He was the calm one now and I was tense.

"Get in the car," he said. "No homie of mine is taking the bus when it's this cold."

I smiled and nodded, followed him to his car with my hands in my pockets.

Before we got in the car, I spoke up: "I need to know what you meant by that. Back in the gym."

He looked at me with no expression at all on his face. "I meant what I said."

"That he'll mess with my scholarship?"

"Yeah, if you don't do what he say," he said.

I thought about that for a second.

"Yo, can we do this in the car?" he whined. "A nigga will freeze out here in weather like this."

"I need to know," I demanded.

"Look," he said. "Things are going fine now

between you and Coach. I can tell that. But the deadline is coming up. And if you don't do what he wants you to do . . . "

"What do you mean?" I said, and then I thought about the list in my pocket, the list that Coach gave me.

Terrell didn't say anything. He didn't need to.

"Come on," I said. "Let's go."

We got into his car and Terrell raced out of the parking lot.

SEVEN

Robin and I planned on meeting at the mall that following Sunday. We said we'd see a movie and maybe get something to eat, but I didn't really care what we did as long as we hung out. I got there early and walked around the mall for a while, anticipating how it would be when she arrived. I stopped outside of Foot Locker and stared through the glass at a display of Nike basketball shoes. My eyes were fixed on the shoes, but my mind was somewhere else. My college decision weighed on me as the clock was ticking loudly now, and the talk with Terrell about Coach didn't help with clearing the matter up in my head.

"Paul," a soft voice said from behind.

I turned around and saw Robin standing there. She smiled, telling me that she was happy to see me. I was definitely happy to see her. Anytime she was around, even if it was just during class or for five minutes in the hall, the pressure in my life seemed to melt away.

"Are you dreaming about your future?" she said, nodding to the shoes behind the glass.

I chuckled. "I know not to get my hopes up."

"Why do you say that?"

"Because I know you can plan on things happening in life a certain way and then they turn out different."

"You don't believe in destiny then?"

"I don't."

We walked to the food court side by side. I didn't feel uncomfortable when there wasn't anything to say. I just waited until there was. We got some Chinese food and sat down at a table across from each other.

"What is your most favorite thing about basketball?" she said.

"I thought you hate sports."

"I do," she said. "But I want to know why you love basketball."

I had to think on that for a moment. I didn't want to give her the played out "love of the game, love of competition" answer. I really didn't know why I loved basketball because I had never really thought about the game in terms of love. I just played it for as long as I could remember. I wasn't even sure that I did love it.

"I don't know," I said. "I'm good at it. So I just keep doing it."

"That's it?"

"Yeah. I guess."

A dubious look came onto her face as she took a sip of her soda.

"What about you?" I asked. "What do you love?"

She put her cup down and looked at me before speaking. Her light eyes became intense in an instant. As if I had asked her the most personal question there was.

"It's too stupid," she said. "You don't wanna hear it."

"Yes I do."

"No, no, no."

"Tell me."

She smiled again, this time her cheeks flushed. "Dogs."

"Dogs?" I said.

"Yeah. I want to be a vet."

"Why is that stupid?" I said.

"I don't know, people in Inglewood don't really get it."

"That's really cool," I said. Then I thought my answer regarding my love of basketball was stupid.

"Do you have a dog?" I asked.

"No, we don't have enough room at my mom's apartment. It's not fair to the dog."

I nodded and took a sip from my soda.

"I volunteer three times a week at a shelter in

Inglewood. On Saturdays we try to find homes for abused pit bulls."

"They get a bad rap, right?"

"Yeah, people think they are vicious just because there are assholes out there that make them fight," she said. "As soon as someone sees a pit bull, they are against them. They might not say it out loud. But that's what they're thinking."

"So that's what you love?" I said.

She nodded. "We're trying to change people's minds in the community."

"That's a hard thing to do," I said.

"It is."

———

After we ate, we decided to skip the movie and just walk around the mall for a while. We both enjoyed talking to one another and we both felt that sitting silently in a movie theater for an hour and an half would be a huge waste of time.

"Did you decide on where you are going to college?"

"You too?"

"I know you must get that from everyone," she said.

"Yeah, I'm taking my time. Not really sure what I'm looking for to be honest. All the schools are pretty much offering the same thing. I'm hoping I wake up one morning and the decision will come to me."

"Life doesn't work like that, Paul."

"I know it doesn't," I said. "That's why I said I hoped."

"As much I dislike sports," she said. "You have talent. And it's hard out there."

There was a feistiness to her that I loved. She didn't go along with things to keep the peace like most people. She had to believe it to go along with it. And if she had an opinion on something, she'd most definitely share it with you. I really liked that about her.

"Can I ask you something, Robin?"

"Yeah."

"Why do you hate sports so much?"

She stopped walking and I did the same. Out of nowhere, her eyes started to water around the edges. She took a tissue from her purse and dabbed at the edges of her eyes.

"Robin, I'm sorry if my question—" I said.

"No, it's not you," she said, with a suddenly stuffy nose. "My brother was a star basketball player at Watts High School. He had his pick of any college on the West Coast. He committed to USC though."

She started walking again and I caught up with her.

"When he was a senior he went to homecoming with his date and a group of friends. They were leaving the parking lot after the dance and this car pulled up and opened fire on my brother, two of his friends, and their dates. The six of them were dead on the spot. It turned out that the shooting was revenge."

I tried to swallow the lump in my throat but it was no use. "Revenge for what?" I said weakly.

"The one who shot my brother was his date's ex," she said as her eyes welled up again. "My brother didn't even know him. He was just minding his business, leaving the dance with his friends."

"How old were you?" I said.

"Ten," she said, after a few sniffles. "My brother was eight years older than me."

"Were you close to him?"

"Yeah," she said, putting her head down and holding the tissue to her eye. "Things were better when he was alive. After he died, my mom went downhill."

"I'm sorry, Robin."

"When it doesn't hurt too much, my mom tells me stories about him. To fill in what I don't remember about how he was."

"I know."

"You know what?"

"I know how it works."

She didn't say anything to that, she just eyed me for a while before going to the bathroom to clean herself up. I waited for her, feeling lousy about making her cry. She came out and joined me again.

We walked out of the mall in silence. We were both catching the bus home, hers to Inglewood and mine to Watts. Her eyes had stopped watering by the time her bus approached.

"Just make sure you don't lose track of your dream, Paul," she said, as the bus came to a stop.

She gave me a hug and we said goodbye until Monday in science class.

As I waited for my bus, I thought about Robin's brother and his dream. He didn't lose track of his, to put it in Robin's words. It was snatched away from him. Where we lived, dreams could be lost or stolen. That's probably why most people in South Central didn't dream at all.

EIGHT

The preseason tournament in San Diego pit four of the top high schools in California against each other. We got a chance to play against a team that we wouldn't normally face because they weren't in our section. You qualified for the tournament by having the top regular season record in your section the year before. We had not only qualified for the tournament but also held the number one seed because we won it the year before. We represented Los Angeles, while the three others represented San Diego, Northern California, and the Central Valley. It was a two-day tournament and, if all went well, we would play two games on

Saturday and two more on Sunday in an effort to repeat as tourney champs.

The tournament was known for two things: brutal competition and the large number of scouts in the stands. I was used to scouts being up in the stands, watching me play. They didn't make me nervous, and, the truth of it was, I didn't think about them while I was on the court. My focus was to repeat as champs.

Our first game was with the team from Central Valley, a Catholic school from Fresno with a lot of size. They had two, six-foot-ten twins who had committed to Cal. They made life miserable for us in the first half. They blocked ten shots—three of mine—and combined for twenty-two of their team's forty points. They led us by ten at the half.

I had twenty of our thirty-one and Terrell had the other eleven. The locker room was dead quiet as we waited for Coach to give us his adjustments. I looked around at the guys' faces and I didn't like what I saw. I had to say something.

"You guys scared?" I said, after standing up. My voice rang off the walls and the sound of it was dramatic because of how quiet it was there.

No one answered. Not even Terrell. They just stared back at me. I think they were shocked because I had never done this before. Coach was standing in the corner, and I could see he had a smile on his face.

"If you guys are scared," I said. "Just give me the ball and get out of my way."

Still nothing.

"I don't care how tall they are," I said. "If I drive the lane and it's open, take it strong!"

Coach walked up next to me.

"And if not," I said. "Kick it back out."

"Paul's right," Coach said. "We can't hesitate with these two big guys. No pump-faking. No floater. Gotta take it strong."

Coach didn't have much in the way of adjustments and sent us out to warm up for the second half. I had an adjustment and I waited behind in the locker room to share it with Coach.

"Coach," I said. "Let's set our pick-and-rolls out higher. And when they switch, I can attack one of the twins with my speed."

"How do you see that working?" he said.

"It'll take one of them out of the paint," I said. "It's hard down there with both of them. But we get one of them out and it'll open things up."

"Let's try it," he said.

When we got back onto the floor for the second half, my suggestion worked. Each time we ran the high pick-and-roll, I attacked one of the twins with my speed and when the second twin stayed in the paint, I pulled up for an uncontested mid-range jumper. I hit six out of ten on those in the second half. When they adjusted and the second twin jumped out to stop me, I just dropped the ball off to an open teammate underneath for a layup or an open shooter for a corner three. I had eight assists in the second half to go along with fifteen points.

Our defense picked up as well in the second half. We didn't like to bring the double team much because when you do, you run the risk of compromising your entire defense. But with the twins causing as much havoc as they did in the first half, we had no other choice. We changed it up, coming with aggressive double teams anytime the twins caught the ball in the post. We mixed up our coverages on them too, confusing them as to where the double was coming from. Terrell collected four steals in the second half and deflected at least five more. I used my length to get into the passing lanes after the twins were doubled and collected three steals of my own.

In the fourth quarter, when we had wrested control of the game, there was a defining sequence. They were in possession of the ball, down twelve, on life support. After trapping one of the twins on the baseline, he somehow found his brother underneath the basket for an apparently easy finish. I hit the jets, elevated, and blocked the twin's dunk attempt from behind. He never saw me coming. The block ignited our fast break going the other way and Deonte finished it with a powerful, two-hand dunk that sent our fans into a frenzy and capped a fifteen-zero run in our favor. They called a timeout. The twins shook their heads in unison. Game over.

We won the game seventy-five to fifty-five. I finished with thirty-five points, eleven boards and nine assists. Defense like that would get us to ARCO. Defense like that causes slumped shoulders for the other team. It's hard to sustain defense like that. It hurts to play defense like that. Defense isn't pretty. It doesn't get you recruited. It just gets you wins.

———

I saw Coach in between games. He went up into the stands and chatted with a few scouts. Out of the corner of my eye, I saw them pointing at me, discussing my future. Coach only talked to three scouts. No surprise that they were from the three schools that were on the list that he gave me.

Terrell's warning lingered in my mind. I knew this situation with Coach was going to be something that I had to deal with. But I still had a little time. And besides, I wanted to give everything I had to my teammates.

I put it out of my head and focused on the next game.

———

Our second opponent in the tournament was the team from Northern California, a public school from Oakland.

We started out fast, jumped on them early. I took control in the middle of the first quarter, scoring nine points in a row and setting the tone defensively. I finished the first half with thirteen points, four rebounds, eight assists, and those two blocks.

We led by fifteen at the half.

The second half was no different. They didn't make any adjustments and we continued shredding them offensively with good ball movement and smart cuts. The biggest play of the second half came when we were up twenty in the fourth quarter. I stole the ball and pushed it ahead. Terrell raced downcourt, joining me on a two-on-one fast break. When the defender committed to me, I threw a lob to Terrell that he dunked with two hands. I knew he could jump, but I didn't think he could get up there like that. It was a loud exclamation point for a dominating wire-to-wire victory.

After the final buzzer sounded, Terrell ran over to me and we both jumped into the air for an emphatic chest bump, followed by a high five that still stings my hand when I think about it.

"I didn't think you were gonna get up there to get it!" I yelled.

He nodded like a madman, adrenaline pumping through his veins.

"Just throw it up there, son!" he said. "I'll go and get it!"

With our two victories, we were guaranteed a

spot in the championship game on Sunday afternoon. But we wanted to get the last round-robin game against the team from San Diego too. We wanted to win every time we stepped on the floor.

———

Back at the hotel, I couldn't sleep. Terrell crashed out in the other double bed right after dinner. He said that he wanted to be fresh for the championship game. That was a far cry from the Terrell of just one year before, who snuck out of the hotel and into the San Diego night after curfew.

I was wide awake though. I missed my parents and my sister. But that wasn't anything new. I would always miss them, for the rest of my life. I missed my grandmother too. I called the house after the game to check up on her. I told her that she didn't have to wait up for me. She told me that she would anyway. Then I thought about Robin and her brother. I really enjoyed spending with her the week before. Even though my team-mates would talk shit if I told them that I didn't even kiss her. I picked up the hotel phone and called her cell phone, even though I didn't really have anything to say to her in particular. I just wanted to call her and say hello. I just wanted to hear her voice.

She didn't pick up and it went to her voicemail. I didn't plan on leaving a message but when I heard the beep, I just started talking.

"Hi Robin, it's Paul. I'm in the hotel right now and I just wanted to say hi, see how you are doing."

I paused.

"I feel like I owe you something. When I was five, my parents and older sister were killed in a car accident. It's been just me and grandmother ever since. I know how you feel. If you get this before tomorrow morning and you want to talk, call the hotel's number and dial three-oh-five for the room number. Good night, Robin."

I don't know why I did it. It felt fair. I felt squared with her.

———

Robin called in the morning before I went to breakfast. She said that my message was one of the sweetest things anyone has ever done for her. I didn't know that I did anything for her but accepted the compliment anyway.

"Even though I hate sports," she said, "good luck out there today."

"Thanks," I said.

We hung up.

It was a good start to what I hoped would be a good day.

If we beat the team from San Diego in the last round-robin, we would play the team from Oakland again in the final. If San Diego beat us, we'd play them again in the championship game. We didn't really have a preference on who we wanted to face. Finishing the weekend undefeated was most important to us.

The game against San Diego started as a back-and-forth contest. It was a morning game and my legs felt tight. Both teams started slow offensively, missing a lot of open shots and the score was tied at sixteen after one. Terrell exploded in the second quarter for fifteen points. Most of the damage was done while I was on the bench. Coach took me out two minutes into the quarter and it was the right move. I cheered on my teammates from the bench as they opened up a twelve-point lead by halftime.

"I want to rest you in the second half for the championship game, Paul," Coach said in the locker room at half time.

"I'm okay, Coach. Really."

"Bobby!" Coach said, looking over my shoulder. "I want you to look at Paul's ankle."

Bobby was our trainer.

"I'm fine, Coach," I pleaded. "I would let you know if I wasn't."

"I know it's not a big thing, Paul," he said. "I just want to make sure you're alright for the long haul. This is just the beginning of our journey."

"I can play."

"We'll finish them without you. And you'll be fine for the final this evening," he said, with a smile and a wink before walking away.

Bobby sat me down, took the tape off of my left foot and asked me where it was sore.

Terrell came over and put a hand on my shoulder.

"You a'ight?" he said.

"I'm good, just a li'l sore is all."

"I got this," he said.

"It's all yours," I said.

We blew them out in the second half. Coach went with a full-court trapping defense in an effort to cause turnovers and speed up the game. Terrell had a lot steals and deflections on defense in the second half. Too many to even count. What made his defensive performance even more impressive was the fact that he poured in twenty-two, second-half points on offense. I was his biggest supporter on the bench, standing up to wave my warm-up shirt every time he made a big play. He finished the game with thirty-eight points and suddenly it wasn't a given that I was going to take home the tournament MVP trophy. Seeing Terrell play like that just made me want to get out there even more. We were all having a blast and it showed. Every player on the team, no matter how much or how little they played, was pulling for one another. And if we kept it that way, we couldn't be stopped.

It was us against Oakland in the championship game. North versus South. There was no way I was going to miss it.

———

Coach came into the locker room before the championship game and sat down next to me as Bobby re-taped my ankle.

"I'm really impressed with how you were pulling for your teammates after I sat you down."

"No doubt," I said. "That's big for us. To play like that when I'm not out there."

"How's the ankle?"

"Fine," I said. "I'm about to go get a little work-out. Get some shots up."

"Okay," he said. "Take Bobby with you."

"Okay."

My ankle was fine after my workout and I was excited and a little relieved to get back on the floor with my team. Excited because it was the final game of the tournament. Relieved because I didn't want Terrell getting too comfortable as the focal point of the team.

After one half of the championship game, we were up by one point, fifty to forty-nine. Terrell stayed hot from the game before and finished the half with fifteen. I was more of a decoy on the offensive end, finishing with ten points and five assists. Our defense stunk in the first half. Oakland played much harder than the first time too. They wanted to pay us back for embarrassing them.

I went to Coach out on the floor before the start of the second half. I worried that Terrell was using up too much energy on both ends of the floor.

"Put me on their best player," I said, referring to Oakland's point guard.

"Your ankle," he said. "And we're gonna need your offense in the second half."

"I'm gonna guard him with or without your permission, Coach," I said.

"Can you handle the load?" he yelled, as the cheerleaders from Oakland pumped up their cheering section. "I mean, I know you can handle the load on a normal day. But today ain't normal with the ankle."

"I got it."

"You sure?"

I nodded. There wasn't anything more to say.

We opened the second half with a quick burst. The decision to put me on their point guard rattled them and their offense. They responded with a run of their own to tie the score at seventy-five as the quarter ended.

In the fourth quarter, I started off the ball on offense to conserve energy for the defensive side. Terrell handled the ball and we went to our one-two set on every possession, where I set a screen for his man in order to force a smaller defender to switch out on me. It worked because when they brought the aggressive double to me, I was able to see over the smaller defender and find the open man. We scored on five straight possessions like this.

On the defensive end, I slowed their point guard down, but that just opened it up for other players on their team. The fatigue of four games and two days was setting in for us. My ankle throbbed a little more with every cut and jump. I put my hands on my knees for the first time in a long time.

With one minute to go, the score was tied at eighty-six. They hit two free throws to go up by two. We called timeout.

Coach ordered us to dig deep in the huddle. He yelled over both cheering sections as best as he could, but it was hard to hear him.

"If you don't have the ball," he screamed, "make sure you move! I don't wanna see anybody standing around! And set some screens, goddammit!"

We broke the huddle and I was as calm as could be. The game didn't rattle me.

We inbounded the ball and Terrell held it up top. Deonte set a pin-down screen for me to get free and receive the ball. Terrell threw a dangerous pass that was almost deflected, but I caught it at the left elbow, foul line extended. There was no double team yet, but all five of their players had their eyes on me. They were waiting for me to make my move. I took one dribble to the left and all five defenders took a step to the left. There were no clear passing lanes. I couldn't find an easy pass that would lead to an easy bucket. Terrell clapped for the ball at the top of the key. But I ignored him. Sometimes the game gives you a riddle with no clear answer.

I kept my dribble alive and squared up. I knew they weren't going to let me get into the paint and that I was going to have to beat them with a jumper. I took two hard dribbles to the left and pump-faked forcefully. My defender, thinking that I was actually shooting, left his feet. When I saw him in the air, I re-cocked quickly and let the shot go. The defender clipped my legs with his hip as he flew by. I hit the deck. The shot rattled in. The whistle blew. And one. I hit the free throw. We were up one: eighty-nine to eighty-eight.

They called a timeout.

There were thirty seconds to go.

During the timeout, I couldn't hear anyone talk in the huddle. I couldn't hear the crowd noise. I was locked in. I was engaged. I felt at peace.

We broke the huddle and they inbounded the ball to their point guard. He brought the ball across half court and kept it there with his dribble alive. He was going to hold it for the last shot. He was going for the game winner.

I just waited for him at the three-point line. I looked back quickly for the screens, but they never came. It was me against him. He thought he could beat me with his speed, that he didn't need any help to get by me.

With ten seconds left, he attacked. He went right and crossed over to his left. But I stayed on him. He kept his dribble alive and reset. There had to have been only five seconds left but I stayed in my defensive stance. My ankle burned but I ignored it.

He attacked again, he stepped back for the game-winning jump shot. I stretched my left arm out as far as I could to contest the shot and I got a fingernail on the ball. The shot fell short. The buzzer sounded. My teammates tackled me. It was hard to get any air underneath. It was humid inside the gym.

But somehow, it was all beautiful.

When I got up off the ground and took some air into my lungs, Coach was there with a fatherly smile. He didn't say anything. There was nothing to say. He just gave me a big hug.

I took the MVP trophy for the tournament, my second in two years.

On the bus ride back to LA, Terrell and I sat in the back by ourselves, while the rest of the guys were up front laughing and singing. To them, it was as if we won the state championship. But to Terrell and me, the two seniors on the team, the win was already in the rearview. The season was long.

Terrell didn't say anything about having to switch defensive assignments with me. He didn't complain about me waving him off during our last offensive possession of the game. He had matured a lot from the season before.

He tapped me on the shoulder and I stood up and turned around.

"What's up?" I said.

"You see Coach up in the stands?" he said, with sleep in his eyes. "With the scouts?"

I nodded.

"Somethin's up," he said.

I didn't say anything to that.

"You better sign somewhere soon," he said, "or he's gonna make the decision for you."

And with that, Terrell sunk down into his seat and closed his eyes. I turned back around in my seat, but didn't close my eyes. Thoughts raced through my mind fast, like the cars next to us on the 5. Too fast to catch a good sleep.

NINE

"Take a seat, Paul," Coach said in his office after Thursday's practice, one day before the season opener.

"I gotta get home, Coach," I said. "It's late and my grandmother isn't feeling well."

"It'll only take a second," he said.

I took a seat.

"How's the ankle? You can rest tomorrow. We need you healthy for the whole season."

There was no way in hell I was missing the first game of the season.

"It's fine," I said. "Those couple of days off from practice helped."

"Good," he said, nodding. "Good."

He sighed, then took his glasses off, and rubbed the bridge of his nose. He tossed them onto his desk.

He sat there silent and I did too. We stared at each other for a moment. It was uncomfortable because I knew what was coming. Coach had this look on his face like something heavy was on his mind. As for me, time was running out and I didn't have the luxury of waiting anymore.

"Did you look at the list, Paul?" he finally said.

"Yeah."

"What did you think?"

Now I sighed and shifted in my chair.

"I have a list of three schools too," I said in a low voice.

"And?"

"None of the ones that are on your list are on mine," I said.

He leaned back in his chair and eyed me without blinking. It was clear that he was the one who had the experience at this. I felt nervous because I was out of my comfort zone. On the court, I knew what to expect. Making the right decision of choosing a college was more difficult and stressful than I could've ever imagined and I had no one at home to help me with it. The only person I had was Coach.

"Well, I'm gonna tell you what you're gonna do, Paul," he said, with serious eyes. "You're gonna pick one of the schools on the list that I gave you."

"They're not on my list, Coach," I said.

"You're gonna pick one of those, Paul," he said. "I don't really care which one."

I couldn't believe what was happening. I thought that Coach was the one person other than my grandmother that I could trust.

He shrugged his shoulders and said, "And that'll be the end of it."

The tone in his voice was one I didn't recognize. He usually talked to me like a friend would. Or perhaps how a father would. But this was different. He talked down to me. Like he owned me.

Coach put his glasses back on and picked up a sheet of paper from his desk.

"Now get on home," he said, without looking up. "It's late."

There were a lot stories out there about star basketball players and the troubles they faced when deciding on where to go to college. There was the usual: shady AAU coaches, agents, and greedy family members. I had never heard of a coach forcing a player to go one college over another, though. But that's what was happening to me. And Terrell's words of warning came back and rang in my ears.

"No," I said.

Coach put the paper down and his eyes focused on my response.

"No?"

"I won't go to any of those," I said, standing up.

Coach stood up and walked around his desk. He approached me and got in close.

"How quickly you forget?" he said.

"What?"

"All the things I've ever done for you."

I didn't say anything and instead tried to back away from him and out of the office. He grabbed me by the shoulder to stop me from leaving.

"You know what I had to do to get you eligible to come here and play basketball?" he said. "You think you'd have Division I scholarship offers if you attended any of those shitty schools in Watts?"

"Coach, I appreciate—"

"No," he said, raising his voice. "I found you. I made it happen. Without me, there is no you. And let's not forget your little problem last year that I got rid of for you."

I could sense that he was trying to intimidate me. And he succeeded. I couldn't look him in the eye.

"It's time to get what's coming to me," he said.

I looked up at him, but couldn't say anything. He had me where he wanted me.

"I didn't want it to be this way," he said, "but you forced my hand, Paul."

I backed away from him and left the office. I quickly made my way out of the school and when the crisp air hit my face, I zipped up my jacket and pulled my hood over my head in self-defense. I walked to my first bus stop and as I waited a sickness sloshed around in the pit of my stomach. In an instant, I felt it start to come up and I did my best to turn around and get it all into a garbage can. I pulled my head out of the can and gasped for clean air. I spat on the street a few times to get the sour taste out of my mouth, but it was no use. I looked around to see if there was anyone there watching, witnessing my breakdown, but there wasn't.

It was the most alone I had ever felt in my life and that was something, seeing as I had a life that was based on being alone.

———

When I got off the first bus, I decided to walk home instead of waiting for the second one. I didn't feel like waiting around; I needed to do something to clear my head, even if it was the simple act of walking. Besides, I didn't want my grandmother to see me upset, because if she knew I was upset, she'd get upset.

As I walked down Florence, the anger continued to bubble inside of me. The run-down, vacant houses and littered sidewalks didn't help to raise my spirits. A siren wailed and a police car ripped past me down the street through a red light.

My ankle started to act up and I stopped to take a break at the corner of Florence and Fifth. There were some people, most of them homeless, walking around. A guy that didn't look to be homeless leaned on a lamp post, eyeing me. He approached me after a little while. He had a red baseball hat on.

"Hey, you up?" he said. "I got dimes for ten. Two of 'em for fifteen. Coke or ice, whatever you need."

When I got a closer look at him, I realized that he was an old friend that I grew up with. He lived in the house three doors down from me. I hadn't seen him since seventh grade.

"Is your name Mike?" I said.

"Yeah," he said. "Who's asking?"

He raised the bottom of his black hoodie and revealed the gun in his waistband. The handle had a red bandana wrapped around it.

"I'm just asking because I think we used to be friends," I said. "You grew up on Crenshaw, near Seventy Third, right?"

I slowly pulled my hood down so he could see my face.

His demeanor changed. He dropped his hoodie back down and a smile came onto his face.

"Paul?" he said.

"Yeah, what's up, man?"

We shook hands complete with a half-hug.

"This nigga," he said. "I've been following you

on the court. I know you're ballin' out over there at Inglewood."

"Yeah, well, you know," I said. "How you been? Why'd you leave after seventh grade?"

"Aw, man. My mom, you know, she got strung out. Lost the house. And I had to go live with my uncle over on Slauson and Normandie."

He shrugged his shoulders.

"And, you know, since then, I've just been hustlin'," he said.

Seeing people hustling out on the corners was a common thing in Watts. Most of my friends who weren't athletes hustled because they had to do something to get by. When you drop out of school in South Central LA, there's a good chance you'll be out there hustling in no time. I understood it and didn't judge it. But seeing Mike out there gave me a different kind of feeling. He was my first friend. Not only did we come up in the same neighborhood, we also shared similar circumstances—loss of parents through tragedy. And, although we hadn't seen each other for a few years, it hurt a little to see him out there. I saw how our lives were running side by side for awhile before our paths changed course. The destinations couldn't have been more different.

"But how you been?" Mike said. "You gonna be gettin' up out of here soon. Big timin' it and shit?"

"I'm just," I said. "I'm just trying . . ."

I didn't know what to say.

Mike stared at me and it was clear that neither of us had anything else to say. The divide between us was huge. You didn't have to be educated to see it. It was right there.

"I gotta roll," I said.

"A'ight," he said. "It was good seeing you. Say hi to your grandmama for me. And stay up, nigga. Keep doin' your thing."

We shook hands again, along with the half-hug.

"Thanks man," I said. "Take care of yourself out here."

He nodded and walked back over to his spot under the lamp post.

I continued home. I put the situation with coach out of my head and I thought on the old days instead. Mike was the first friend I played basketball with. Every day, after school, I'd knock on his door to get him to come to the courts with me, and, from what I could remember, he wasn't much of a player. He was good at math though. I bet that served him well out on the corner.

TEN

As I walked through the halls for my first class on Friday morning, I could feel the energy and excitement of the new season. Our gym, during home games, was always packed, and this year would be no different. But with excitement came pressure. Pressure on the team to deliver a state championship. Pressure on me to lead us there. The feelings were raw from the night before. I was angry because I felt that Coach had betrayed me. But I had to put it out of my head, at least until after the game.

I couldn't focus in class. There were so many things swirling through my mind: the first game of the season, Coach's ultimatum. The first couple periods flew by and I couldn't name one thing that the teachers talked about. But I did look forward to third period because that meant seeing Robin. I planned to ask her if she wanted to come to the game and then hang out after. I was eager to have her see me play in person.

The only problem with my plan was that she wasn't in class. I talked to her the day before in class and she didn't say anything about missing school the next day. She didn't look sick. I asked a couple people in class if they saw Robin during the earlier class periods, but they said they didn't. I was worried about her and in between classes, I borrowed Terrell's cell phone to call her. Her phone didn't ring and I didn't leave a message because I didn't want her calling Terrell's cell phone back.

The rest of the day went by and I didn't see Robin in the halls. I tried calling her again and got the same result. Her absence was strange. I hoped that she was okay.

The game was about an hour away and the gym was already packed and buzzing. I usually didn't spend much time scanning the crowd as I warmed up. I never did. But tonight, I wanted to see which scouts were in attendance. I saw scouts from the three schools on Coach's list, along with a couple from my list.

I avoided Coach in the locker room before the game and he did the same with me. I wanted to keep what was going on between us, because I didn't want it to affect my game and I didn't want the other guys to know. I didn't know what his intentions were, just like I didn't know that he had his own plan for which college I was going to attend. Our only interaction came right before the tip when he told me, "Lead us." I turned to the rest of the guys without acknowledging him. He didn't deserve my respect anymore. I felt a responsibility to my teammates and myself. No one else.

The referee tossed the ball up into the air and the new season was officially underway. We took a quick ten-point lead after one quarter. I finished the quarter with fifteen points, a few boards, three assists, and a couple of blocks. Coach took me out at the beginning of the second because of the lead and I needed it, because the ankle was a little tender. Also, I wanted to see how the team reacted with me on the bench. I rested the entire second quarter and we took a twenty-point lead into the locker room at the half.

The third quarter was no different. I had ten more points along with the play of the game at the end of the quarter. With just five seconds left in the frame, I stole the ball at half-court and raced down to the other end for a ferocious one-handed slam at the buzzer. As I went up in the air for the dunk, the flashbulbs from the photographers underneath the basket blinded me, causing me to finish the play with my eyes closed. I glared at the photographer after the play and Coach tried to calm me down on the bench in between quarters. But I just kept ignoring him. The photographers on the baseline were the worst. Playing the game was hard enough, playing it without being able to see was something ridiculous.

I didn't play in the fourth quarter. None of our starters did. Our backups held the lead, extending it to thirty at one point, and we cruised to our first victory of the season. It was hopefully the first of many and according to the *LA Times*, the first of a thirty-and-O season.

I finished with thirty points, ten boards, six assists, three steals, and three blocks.

Five reporters surrounded me on the floor after the game. None of my other teammates—even Terrell, who'd had a monster game himself—were approached by a single reporter. I didn't have anything for them. It was a blowout win in the first game of the season against a lesser opponent. What's there to say? What's there to analyze? But that's not what they were there for. They wanted to know my college decision. They wanted to be the first to break the news.

"Guys," I said, with five tape recorders in my face. "When I have a decision, I'll let you guys know. I just want to enjoy this season with my teammates. Enjoy this ride."

And with that I escaped out of the semi-circle of reporters and made my way to the locker room. The attention I got from the reporters didn't bother the rest of the team. That included Terrell, who went back to his normal self after our rocky exchange over the *Times* article. I thought that, in a way, the rest of the guys welcomed how much attention I received because it took pressure off of them.

By the time I got back there, Coach had already talked to the team. I was glad I missed it. The guys didn't notice anything. The locker room was the same as it always was after wins—music blasting, laughing, hollering, shit talking. Most of the guys were already showered and changed, ready to go have fun and celebrate the win in pairs or small groups.

"That dunk is gonna be all over YouTube by tomorrow morning, Paul," Deonte said, as I walked past him to my locker. "Watch."

I smiled at him in response. The rest of the guys laughed and made comments, affirming Deonte's claim. I got a handshake or pat on the back from every teammate before I sat down in front of my locker, took a deep breath, and closed my eyes for a little bit. By the time I opened them, the room was quiet. Everyone was gone except for Terrell.

Terrell sat down next me. He put a diamond earring into each one of his ears. I thought about Robin and wondered if she was okay.

"Lemme use your phone," I said.

He took his cell phone and handed it to me. UCLA was paying for that, too.

"Who you calling?" he said.

"Robin."

He nodded.

Still no answer. I didn't leave a message. I handed the phone back to Terrell.

"You comin', son?"

"Where?"

"Party, up in the Hollywood Hills."

"Ah—"

Coach entered into the locker room.

"Paul, I need you in my office," he said.

I shook my head.

"Now!" he yelled.

"Give me a second," I said.

He left the locker room and went back into his office. I stood up and put a shirt on.

"Fuck is up with him?" Terrell said, while scanning through the messages in his phone.

I eyed the hallway that led to Coach's office.

When I got to it, someone else was in there with Coach. The man was sitting across from Coach at his desk, with his back to me. They were talking. I knocked on the doorframe and Coach looked up at me. The man turned his head and I quickly recognized him. He was a scout from one of the colleges on Coach's list. He had come to every one of my games last year. I had never talked to him because I never seriously considered going to the school he represented.

"Sit down, Paul," coach said.

I stood in the doorway, ignoring his order.

The scout kept his eyes on me. Coach gestured to him.

"I want you to—"

"No," I said, sternly. "This is against the rules."

Coach looked at the scout and they both smiled.

"Okay," Coach said. "It's alright. No one here is going to say anything to anybody."

"I'm not going to be a part of this," I said, before taking a step out of the office.

"Paul," Coach said.

I walked away. I turned my back on Coach and walked away. He called my name one more time and then silence. The scout and Coach didn't exchange any words as I walked down the hall, away from the office. They were stunned.

I went straight to the shower and got in and out

of there. When I got back to my locker, Terrell was still there alone.

"What did Coach say?" he said.

"Did he come into the locker room while I was in the shower?" I said. "With some guy?"

"Nah," he said. "Why?"

I looked at the hallway that led to Coach's office, and then at Terrell.

"I'll tell you when we get outside," I said. "I need to get out of here."

I changed clothes just as fast as I had showered.

"So you're coming to the party?"

I shook my head. "I'm not."

"This is our last year," he said, with persistence. "And since you being all secretive and shit about where you going to college, I bet you're probably leaving LA."

"I haven't decided that yet," I said.

"Whatever," he said. "We don't have many more chances to kick it. Season is only gonna get tougher, won't have easy ones like tonight."

I needed to talk to Terrell about what was going on with Coach. He would understand because he had been through it.

"Okay," I said. "Let's go."

"My nigga," he said, with a smile.

ELEVEN

Terrell sped down the freeway at eighty miles per hour. His car was fast like he was and I could tell that he loved speed, perhaps even needed it. Whether it was playing fast, driving fast or living fast, Terrell had to move at a quicker pace than the rest of us. He chose UCLA without thinking too much about it. Maybe it was because they offered the car? But maybe it was something else? Maybe he needed to make a quick decision because it fit right in to the rest of his fast life? Whatever the case was, he seemed comfortable in his decision to stay home. I, on the other hand, liked to take my time, live at a steady pace. But time was running out and I could feel the pressure from all angles.

"Would you slow down?" I said, over the blaring music. "You're gonna get us pulled over. End it all for us."

"You need to relax some," Terrell said. "I mean, if you don't, you're gonna miss out on all the fun."

"I need to tell you what's going on with Coach," I said, after turning the radio off. "You're the only one I can bring this to."

"Yeah, that's right," he said. "Go ahead."

"Coach told me that I have to choose one of the schools that he picked out for me," I said. "He gave me a list. And when I told him no, he started with the threats."

Terrell had a knowing smile on his face. Like he was a veteran of this game that I was still learning about.

"I told you," he said. "Coach is gonna get his way—one way or another. He got paid off from me committing to UCLA."

"He did the same to you?" I said. "He gave you a list?"

"Not exactly," he said. "But when UCLA started showing a little interest, Coach got himself a little something in exchange for my commitment."

"But I thought you wanted to go to UCLA all along?"

"I did," he said, changing lanes wildly and ignoring the horns and glares of angry drivers who passed us on both sides. "Shit, all this talking made me miss the exit."

"Where is the party?" I said.

"Up in the Hills," he said, with a wide grin. "Hollywood."

"Get back to what you were saying," I said.

"Oh yeah. It ain't nothin' too special. Once Coach found out that I was interested in UCLA and they were interested in me, he made a call."

"And?"

"And they hooked it up," he said.

I didn't say anything.

"You best believe Coach is gonna try to get paid off your letter of intent," he said. "With the type of player you are . . . " Terrell shook his head. "He's gonna get paid."

———

The party was way up there in the Hills, where the houses were tucked away within the curves. Terrell said an agent who hung around UCLA's players was throwing the party. After taking six or seven curves, I lost count of where we were. Terrell knew, though. We stopped at a gate that protected a huge mansion from the rest of the world. I could hear the party going on behind the gate. Terrell pressed a buzzer on the gate and spoke his name when asked. The gate opened and he pulled up to the mansion and put it in park. A Mexican guy took the car and parked it somewhere else.

We stood there looking at the mansion. Terrell

tapped me on the shoulder and pointed to something behind me.

I turned around to see what it was. It was all of LA, like I had never seen it before. Downtown was lit up in the distance. Cars raced past each other on the numerous freeways. I could even see the ocean out there—way out there. It was black because of the time of night, but I knew it was there. The only part of LA that I couldn't see was South Central. That was the only part of town that seemed to be in darkness.

"Damn," I said. "It's different up here."

"Yeah," Terrell said.

"Are you sure we should be here?" I said.

"Relax," he said. "This guy just wants to talk."

"Talk? To me?"

"Yeah, nigga," he said with a smile. "Don't trip."

We walked through the front door of the mansion and it was filled with people. An even mix of males and females from what I could tell. As we made our way from the front door to what looked like the living room, the music got louder. The lights in that room were turned down and I walked carefully to make sure I didn't run into anyone. I could smell marijuana and beer and mostly everyone you saw was either holding a joint or a cup. We passed through that room and made it to the back patio, where the space opened up a little.

When we got out there, a white man with slick-backed black hair spotted us and stood up from a table that was surrounded by two other men and three white women.

"Terrell," the man said as he shook Terrell's hand and gave him a half-hug.

The man then turned to me and put his hand out.

"It's great to meet you, Paul," he said. "You played like a beast down in San Diego."

"Thanks," I said, feeling a bit uncomfortable from the compliment.

"How many you have tonight?" he said. "Twenty-seven? Twenty-eight?"

"Thirty."

There was a pause in the conversation. The man

stared at me and then Terrell, and said, "Terrell, why don't you go get yourself a drink? Or better yet, see Jeri there. She really wants to meet you and she's thirsty, too."

The man laughed along with everyone at the table—women included. Terrell didn't laugh, but stood there smiling. He slapped me on the back and said, "Just try to relax." He nodded to the man with slicked-back hair and walked over to the table, leaving me there standing. One of the men sitting down handed him a cup. One of the women—Jeri, I assumed—got out of her seat and allowed Terrell to sit down. She sat in Terrell's lap and began whispering into his ear as he took gulps from his drink.

"Walk with me, Paul," the man said.

I followed behind slowly. We stopped at the railing that overlooked another part of LA that I couldn't name.

"My name is David," he said. "I'm an agent. I work with kids like Terrell. Kids like you. To help them with their situation."

"Kids like me?"

"I know you're probably nervous being here," he said. "But you're not doing anything wrong."

"Oh yeah?"

"Yeah," he said.

A blonde woman from inside the mansion approached with two beers. She handed one to David.

"Beer, Paul?" he said.

I shook my head.

"Good kid," he said before nodding to the blonde woman. "Thanks, Chrissy. Bring the kid a Gatorade, will ya?"

She nodded and walked away toward the house.

David stared at Chrissy's backside until she disappeared in the sea of people.

"You just say the word, Paul," he said. "And she's yours."

"I'm okay," I said.

"I know about what happened last year after one of your official visits. The rumor," he shook his head before continuing. "The recruiting game is dirty. Nothing like that will happen here. Anything that happens here will stay here."

"I don't need anything from you," I said. "Terrell just brought me up here. I had no idea."

"Well, you had to know something," he said. "I mean, you know about Terrell. No one is that innocent, Paul."

I didn't say anything to that.

"Just one thing," he said, before taking a sip of his beer. "Can you give me an idea on what you're thinking in terms of colleges? It's getting pretty late in the process."

"I'm taking my time," I said, looking past him at the view.

"Have you thought about skipping college altogether?"

"No," I said.

"The NBA scouts *I've* talked to think you could play right now. Of course, you would need another year to be eligible," he said. "We could showcase you in Europe for a season. Get a bit of cash in your pocket, and then be ready for the draft next year. Have you thought about that?"

It wasn't easy standing there, hearing someone on the outside talk about my future in such a public way. I was getting tired of people talking about my future without my thoughts on it. I needed to do something about that. And soon.

"You could change your situation, Paul. You're grandmother's situation, too."

"I'm not interested," I shot back, louder than I planned to.

David smiled in my face and took another sip of his beer.

"And don't bring my family into this," I warned.

"Fair enough," he said with a pat on my back. "Fair enough, Paul."

I turned around and Terrell had gotten up from the table. He was gone. Jeri, too.

"My home is open to you, Paul," he said. "Enjoy the party."

I waited for Terrell on the balcony for thirty minutes, but there was no sign of him. The party got rowdier the longer it went on. The music seemed to get louder the later it got—an offense that surely would've brought the cops out back home in South Central.

Women came and went with different men. I wasn't envious of that. There might have been a time when I was younger that I would've been. But after surviving the vicious rumor during junior year, I made the decision to never trust a woman who was offered up to me. Terrell didn't agree with that. But it was the right choice for me.

Seeing all of the women at the party took my thoughts to Robin. She wasn't easy like those women. She was the opposite. You had to earn her trust and that's one of the things I liked most about her. That, and her eyes.

I still didn't know if she was okay and I needed to borrow Terrell's phone to call her.

I turned to the table and saw David and his friends taking shots of liquor. They were getting looser with their hands and words. I walked over to the table and David looked up to me with glossy eyes after taking another shot.

"I need to find Terrell," I said.

"He'll be out in just a minute, Paul," he said loudly. "Join us."

"I really need to find him," I said.

"Relax. It'll just be a little longer."

I agreed to sit down for a little bit, but reiterated that I wasn't going to drink. David put his hands up in defeat. I sat down without saying anything to anyone.

David collapsed into his chair after one of the other men lit a cigar for him.

He eyed me. "I know you're having some trouble deciding on a school."

I didn't look at him when I replied, "Who said I'm having trouble?"

"It just the word on the streets," he said.

I chuckled. "Nah, there's no trouble."

"You're talented enough to go straight to the league. Why risk getting injured in college when you won't be there more than a year?"

"I won't be one and done," I said. "College means something to me."

I thought of my parents, my sister.

"That's what they all say," he said, as he ashed his cigar.

I didn't say anything to that.

"Think about it. Everybody would win," he said, almost begging me.

I stood up from the table.

"It's time for me to get up out of here," I said. "Can you get Terrell?"

"Terrell's fine," he said. He nodded to a dark-haired girl at the table. "Tina. Why don't you show your talents to Paul here?" He winked at me. "You two are both talented people. I'm sure you'll get along just fine."

Tina stood up and walked over to me. She put her arm around me and tried to kiss me on the lips. I could smell the liquor and cigarettes on her breath and pulled away.

"He's a shy one, David," she said.

David shrugged.

She rubbed my leg and I squirmed away from her. The people at the table laughed.

"I'm gonna go inside to look for him," I said, standing up from the table. "I gotta get back."

Tina made a sad face and sat back down at the table. She almost tripped on her heels before sitting down.

David raised another shot into the air. "It's your first time being here, Paul."

He took the shot.

"You'll change with more experience," he said. "We all do."

I walked into the house to look for Terrell.

The crowd had thinned out some from before. He wasn't in the living room. I should've known that.

He had to be in one of the bedrooms or bathrooms. But the place was huge. I didn't know where to start. I wandered into the kitchen and stopped at a stairwell that went up to another floor. That was as good a place as any to start. It was quieter up there as the sounds from downstairs were muffled. I turned a corner in a dark hallway and heard a woman sobbing quietly. I stopped in my tracks. I knew if I took another step toward the sound, the outcome would not be good. There were no good outcomes to be had in that place. I thought about what my parents would say if they I knew I was here. Same for my grandmother. And then I thought about my future. It could have all gone up in smoke if I kept walking down that hallway.

I almost walked back downstairs and out of the house.

But I couldn't. I had to see if the woman crying was okay. I couldn't just leave her there.

When I took a couple more steps down the hallway, she stopped crying. She gasped instead. And then it was quiet. The hallway was dark save for a dim, yellow light coming out of a room at the end of it. I walked toward the dim light. I stopped in front of a door that was cracked open.

I took a deep breath.

When I pushed the door open, Jeri was there sitting on the edge of a hot tub, half-naked. She started crying again when she saw me. With the same hushed tone as earlier. The makeup around her eyes had run down and smeared all over her face.

I turned my head to the white bathroom floor and saw Terrell lying there. There was a stream of blood coming from his nose. I got down on my knees and saw foam was coming from his mouth.

His eyes were open.

He was looking right at me.

I put my head to his chest.

There was no sound.

"No, no, no!" I screamed.

I looked at Jeri.

She didn't say anything. She just looked down and kept crying.

I pressed on Terrell's chest and blew air into his lungs. I didn't know what I was doing, but I had seen it on TV. It didn't work.

"No!" I said again. "No!"

My lips were covered in his blood and snot. My eyes started to water and my nose stuffed up. I wiped it with my sleeve and looked down to see it painted in clear red.

I stood up from the floor and grabbed Jeri by the shoulders. "What happened?"

She wiped the snot from her nose and stopped crying long enough to say, "I don't know, I . . . he said he just had to puke. He said that he could handle it. He said that it wasn't too much for him."

She looked down again.

I lifted her face up to mine and shook her. "What?" I yelled. "What did he take?"

She broke down and began crying uncontrollably.

I helped her to her feet. We had to get out of here. I had to tell David. I held Jeri up as we walked down the dark hallway. Every moment from my life seemed to race through my head during that slow walk. At the end of the hallway, my mind rested on a single thought: one moment could change everything.

When we got downstairs, the house was pretty much empty, with a few people here and there passed out. I sat Jeri down on a couch in the living room and walked out to the patio, straight to David. He saw that my shirt was covered in blood and he got up from the table and approached me. His steps were wobbly, but his eyes focused at the sight of trouble.

"Why is your shirt covered in blood?"

"Terrell," I said, in a low voice.

He ran his hand through his hair and swayed a bit. He stunk of liquor.

"He's upstairs in your bathroom," I said. "Upstairs in your bathroom. Dead."

I couldn't believe those words coming out of my mouth.

David's shoulders slumped. A sadness came over him.

"Is she up there?" he asked.

"No, she's inside," I said, pointing a thumb behind me.

He sighed and ran his hand through his hair again. Then he rubbed his eyes with his palms and slapped himself in the face a few times.

"You need to get out of here," he said, now alert. "You could lose it all."

This situation was messy and it was only about to get messier. The question now was whether I was going to get caught up in the mess.

"Someone'll get you a ride," he said, as walked past me and into the house.

I walked back inside and went to the kitchen. I stopped at the stairwell that led to the bathroom. But I couldn't walk back up those stairs. Terrell was gone and there was nothing I could do about it.

A black man in a black sports coat and black slacks approached me from behind as I stood there, glued to that spot right in front of the stairwell. He put a hand on my shoulder.

"Let me get you a ride," he said in a deep, listless voice. "Watts, right?"

"Yeah," I said, feeling numb. My head started to throb. My fingers began tingling.

"What happened up there?" he said, nodding to the stairwell.

"You don't know?"

"Uh-uh," he said.

"Terrell," I said. "My teammate. He was up there with a girl. They were snorting something."

"Damn," he said. "That shit's always happening to a brother."

"Can you take me now?" I asked, staring up at the hallway. "I need to get clean. I need to get out of here."

"Let's do it," he said.

TWELVE

The call came early in the morning after a night of troubled sleep. It was Coach. He wanted me to meet him in his office as soon as I could. I told him to give me an hour. I quickly changed clothes, kissed my grandmother on the forehead, and went out to catch the bus.

Coach looked like hell, sitting there behind his desk. I walked inside and took a seat in front of him. His eyes looked heavy, like he had been woken up in the middle of the night.

"Terrell," he said, before pausing. "Terrell died last night. Overdose. They said he thought he was using cocaine, but it was really heroin."

I put a balled fist up to my mouth and opened my eyes wide, but not too wide, to feign surprise. I made sure not to overreact with strong words or over-the-top emotion. Just the balled-up fist. I wanted Coach to do all the talking.

He eyed me carefully.

"Some of the guys," he said. "They said they saw you leave school with him. Did you go to the party with him? I mean, I know you're not into that kind of stuff."

The locker room was empty by the time Terrell and I left for the party. None of my teammates were there to see me leave with Terrell. But Coach said otherwise. That's when I knew that he knew.

"He just took me home, Coach." I said with no expression on my face. "He wanted me to go with him. But I had to get home to my grandmother."

He nodded and sat back in his chair.

"Did he do any drugs in the car on the way to dropping you off at home?"

"No," I said.

"Okay, Paul," he said. "Okay."

"Did you tell anybody else on the team?"

"No, not yet," he said. "I gotta do that."

I didn't say anything.

"Keep this quiet over the weekend, Paul," he said. "The police are involved, they want a lid on it through the weekend. I'll tell the whole team on Monday."

"Okay."

"I'm gonna need you," he said. "More than ever. You're gonna have to pull the guys together."

"Is that all?" I said, standing up from the chair.

"That's all. Do you need a ride home?"

"No."

———

It was nice outside and I decided to walk around a little instead of taking the buses home. I stopped at a diner to get some food and after finishing I used their phone to call Robin's cell phone—her absence from school the day before slipped my mind with all that happened. She picked up this time and I was relieved. I asked her to meet me somewhere in Inglewood and she asked where. When I didn't have a clear meeting place in mind, she said she'd choose one. She said she'd meet me there in fifteen minutes. I hung up the phone, thanked the woman who let me use it, and left the diner. I started walking quickly toward my meeting with Robin. I was excited.

I knew why Coach called me into his office that morning. It wasn't to tell me about Terrell's death. He knew I was there. He called me there to see if I realized what he was up to. For one day at least, he didn't bring up my college decision. But it wouldn't last. Coach was working me again. I just didn't know how it fit into his hustle.

———

I met Robin at the meeting place. It was the animal shelter in Inglewood. She was out front, waiting for me with a stout, brown pit bull on a leash. The dog wagged its tail when I came near. I bent down to pet it and it was more than happy to be pet. When I got a closer look at the dog, I could see all kinds of wounds on its neck and head that seemed to be healing. I felt a big bump behind its right ear as I rubbed it there.

I stood up and gave Robin a hug.

"You're not afraid?" she said.

"Of dogs?" I said. "Nah."

"This is Lucky," she said, nodding down to the dog.

"Lucky, huh?" I said. "Why did you name him that?"

"Because we saved him from some very bad people—that's why."

I smiled at that and so did she.

"Let's take a little walk," she said. "I thought it'd be different to ask you here."

"Okay," I said.

We walked down Crenshaw and the dog led the

way. The people hanging out on the block tensed up when we walked by with Lucky, but the dog didn't pay them any mind. He was enjoying the nice weather and the love from Robin.

"Can you keep a secret?" I said, while Lucky stopped to pee on a fire hydrant.

"Yeah," she said.

"You know Terrell?"

"The one from your team?"

"Yeah."

"What about him?"

"He died."

"He died?"

"Yeah, he overdosed."

"On what?"

"Heroin."

She didn't say anything. We walked in silence until we reached a corner where Lucky stopped to sniff at the air. There were two older men sitting at a table in front of a corner store, drinking beers out of paper bags and playing dominoes.

After a while, I said in a low voice, "I was there."

She looked at me like I was crazy.

"What? Where?"

"This party up in the Hollywood Hills."

She started to roll her eyes, but then she stopped. She caught herself.

"That doesn't sound like you," she said.

"I didn't want to go," I said. "I needed to talk to him about something and I just ended up going with him."

She didn't say anything and we started walking again.

"Can I tell you something else?" I said.

"Yeah."

"I don't really feel bad about it," I said. "I mean, don't get me wrong. I'm not glad he's dead or anything like that. But I'm supposed to feel all sad, right? That's what everyone expects. But I don't."

"Did you know he was using drugs like that?"

"No," I said. "That's the first time we've ever hung out at a place like that."

She didn't say anything as she thought. Lucky stopped again, and we did, too.

"I'm probably still in shock," I said. "I was right next to his body, I had his blood all over my clothes. I'm sure it's going to sink in at some point."

She continued eyeing me.

"But I just don't feel it," I said.

"Are you asking me if it's okay that you don't feel any guilt, Paul?" she finally said.

"I think so," I said.

"You want the truth?"

"Yes."

"It's not on you," she said. "Whenever it sinks in, if it ever does, it still won't be on you."

Hearing her say that made me feel better. I knew deep down that what she said was true. Even before she said it, but it felt good regardless to hear her say it.

"Does your coach know?" she said, as we turned around on Crenshaw and started back to the shelter.

"He knows I was there," I said, "but he's sitting on it."

"On what?"

"The information."

"I don't know what you mean," she said.

"Coach is not looking out for me," I said. "Just like he wasn't looking out for Terrell. Or any other good player he's ever had. Coach looks out for himself first."

Robin looked at me as we got closer to the shelter.

"And now, I'm next," I said. "I'm next in line."

"You're different, Paul," she said.

I bent down one last time to pet Lucky behind his ears.

"Oh yeah, I forgot to ask," I said. "Why weren't you in school yesterday?"

"Yesterday was my brother's birthday," she said. "I couldn't drag myself out of bed. I was too sad."

I stood up. "Today seems to be treating you better," I said.

"Life's like that," she said. "Look at this guy down there."

She nodded down to Lucky and he looked back up to us with his tongue out, smiling.

"Just a few weeks ago, he was being forced to fight other dogs, burned by cigarettes, and you don't even want to know what else."

"But he survived it," I said.

"That's right," Robin said.

THIRTEEN

The school district canceled our games for one week. Coach canceled practice for that week as well. The rest of the guys took it hard because they liked Terrell and he liked everyone else. Being liked wasn't his problem. I worked out after classes every day that week to be ready for the added load on my shoulders when we started playing games again.

I also took the time off to think about my college options. I narrowed my list to two; neither of them were on the list that Coach gave me. I didn't see Coach at all that week. He was busy dealing with the fallout of Terrell's death. But I knew that would change once we got back on the court because there would only be two more weeks to decide on a college. There would be one last battle with Coach over which one I'd choose.

—

When the games started up again, we were dominant. We won four games in a week by an average of twenty-plus points. I scored thirty points a game in that span, and best thing about it was the fact that I did most of my damage from outside of the key. When we had the ball on offense, teams packed the paint because they didn't have to worry about Terrell's dribble penetration or off-the-ball cuts from the weak side. Defenders lagged off of me and made sure to cover the corner shooters. They dared me to beat them from the outside. And I did.

In the fifth game after Terrell's death, Watts High School was our opponent, and they were the team that gave us the only loss in our section from the year before. The game was in their gym and the crowd was hostile—to me especially, because I was the star player that got away from Watts.

The game started out bad for us because I got two fouls early in the first quarter. The second one was questionable at best and I gave the ref a piece of my mind in the form of four-lettered words. He hit me with a technical foul and Coach sat me down with six minutes to go in the first quarter.

Watts finished the quarter on a twelve-O run and we were down by ten after one quarter.

Sitting on the bench allowed me to see things from a different angle. Normally when I came out of the game, Terrell would stay in. We were a much different team without either of us on the floor. Our floor spacing was awful because the other team wasn't threatened by our ball handlers and, on defense, his absence was even more noticeable. The Watt's point guard got them into their offense easily without Terrell there to hassle him full-court.

Watts continued their run, holding us scoreless

at the beginning of the second and went up by twenty around the midway point of the quarter.

Coach called a timeout and put me back into the game. When we broke the huddle, he whistled to me and screamed over the taunting crowd that was now showering us with their own four-lettered words. "Be careful, Paul!" Coach said. "No cheap fuckin' fouls!"

I nodded and walked back onto the floor. I had two goals for the rest of the half: finish with just the two fouls and slash Watts' lead to ten.

I scored three straight baskets upon reentering the game—one of them an emphatic, one-handed slam that quieted the crowd momentarily.

The defensive end was much more difficult, though. I couldn't be aggressive and they continued scoring at a comfortable clip.

With one minute to go in the half, I hit a three to cut the lead to thirteen. But after I made my shot, instead of walking the ball up the floor, Watts pushed it ahead and caught us sleeping. Reacting late, I tried to block the streaking player's layup attempt, but it ended in disaster. He made the layup and I fouled him. I had three fouls at the half. We were down by sixteen.

On the walk to the visitor's locker room, it felt like we were destined to lose. With all of our hard work in the second quarter, we were only able to cut four points off of their twenty-point lead. It was one of those one-step-forward-two-steps-back games. They are the hardest ones to come back and win. But if achieved, they are the sweetest, by far.

Coach didn't say anything to the team in the locker room and neither did I. I knew what I had to do in the second half. I had to go off on both the offensive and defensive ends of the floor. I had to try to find a way to make an impact even though the refs weren't letting me be physical.

Just before walking back out onto the floor, I grabbed Coach and asked him if I could guard the Watts' point guard in the second half. That was the first time in a few weeks that Coach and I actually talked about basketball. Not about college decisions or parties up in the Hills, but basketball. My theory was that even though Watts' best player, Shane Thompkins, was a wing, it would help us out more if I checked their point guard.

Coach didn't agree at first. "We need you on Thompkins! He's their best player!"

"Just hear me out," I said calmly, trying to cool him down, even though I was the one out there playing. "The refs, they're calling it really tight. Let me use my length against the point guard. Try to disrupt their offense that way. It's our only chance."

He thought on it, and said, "Okay. But if Thompkins scores two straight baskets, you're going right back on him."

"Okay."

We hit the floor for the third quarter and the crowd was no less raucous. I started on their point guard and they didn't score on their first five possessions. Like I imagined, my length bothered him and when I picked him up full court, it derailed their offense.

On the other end, we scored on our first six possessions of the quarter. I scored four buckets and assisted on the other two. One of my scores was on a step-back jumper that hit nothing but net and the other three were drives where I forced myself to the basket, basically daring the refs to call an offensive foul. Luckily, they swallowed their whistles on those.

We shaved the lead to seven by the end of the third and it was clear that I was in their point guard's head. He couldn't slash into the paint like in the first half and Thompkins only had two points in the third quarter.

The adjustment continued working for us in the fourth and we played inspired ball on both ends. With a minute to go in the game and the ball in our possession, down by three, coach called a timeout. We had all the momentum. All Watts had was a slight edge on the scoreboard. The mountain top was there. We could all see it.

"Move without the fuckin' ball!" Coach yelled in the huddle. "Paul's gonna break 'em down and when he does, find an open spot! Don't be afraid to take the shot! Have your hands ready and let it fly!"

We all put our hands in the middle.

"This is what it's all about gentleman!" Coach said, like a mad man. "Do it for Terrell! Get to ARCO for Terrell!"

I yelled, "One! Two! Three!"

"ARCO!"

I took the inbound pass and drove straight to the hoop. When a long-armed help defender showed, I had to make a decision. Either pass the ball to a shooter for a contested shot or keep it and try to make something out of nothing?

I faked a pass to a three-point shooter we had planted in the corner. The fake froze the long-armed help defender just long enough for me to find a crease and get to the hoop. As I elevated, their six-foot-eleven center elevated, too, and I knew there would be a mid-air collision. I flicked up a little left-handed shot as Watt's center crashed into me. The shot kissed off the glass and went in. I heard the whistle. I heard the ref yell, "Foul!" I heard our sideline erupt with, "And one!"

And I heard Watts' gym fall into silence.

The sweetest sound in the world.

I knocked in the free throw to tie the game.

Watts called a timeout. The crowd was shell-shocked. No one up there was talking any shit as we stood in the huddle. They knew that I had taken the game over and that it was mine. None of us said anything in the huddle. Just firm high fives, and glares right into each other's eyes. We hadn't done anything yet. We still hadn't climbed the mountain top.

We still had to take our first lead of the game.

But we were right there.

Watts brought the ball in and I picked their point guard up full court. They set a screen in the back court to free him up but I just ran around it and recovered.

By the time he set their play in the front court there was forty-five seconds left to go in the game. He dribbled like he was scared, like he didn't really want to make a move. He didn't want the ball. I had taken his heart.

With thirty seconds to go, they started their action. My teammates yelled out the screens behind me and I turned my head quickly to see what they were trying to run. They wanted to free up their best shooter with a few cross screens along the baseline. I backed off a little to get more depth. The point guard's eyes got big. I knew he was getting ready to pass the ball. When he let it go, I jumped into the passing lane and stretched my left hand out as far it could go. I deflected the ball right into Deonte's hands for the steal. I looked up to the clock and there were fifteen seconds left. I sprinted to Deonte and he handed me the ball. I looked to Coach for the timeout and he didn't say anything. I was happy about that. He didn't need to draw up a play. Everyone in that gym knew who was taking the last shot.

As I raced the ball up the floor, you couldn't hear a sound in that gym. All those crazy, loud people in the crowd were now sitting on their hands like they were in church.

Well, I was about to take them to church.

I attacked the right side with about eight seconds to go. When four defenders converged on me, I found Al open in the corner. He caught the pass with two seconds and let the wide-open three fly.

All I heard after that was *splash*.

Then I heard the buzzer.

Then I heard the crowd gasp.

And suddenly I was underneath a big pile of my teammates. Al and I were somewhere on the bottom of the pile. I could have suffocated and it would've been just fine by me. I couldn't think of a better place to be than at the bottom of that pile.

When I finally got up off the floor and got some air, the bleachers were already thinned out. Coach gave me the biggest hug that I had ever received in my life. He squeezed me so tight that I couldn't breathe. When he let go, he said, "Oh my god! That was beautiful!"

I couldn't speak on it quite yet. The joy inside of me, inside of my teammates, gripped me. I just breathed. And smiled.

Coach shook his head and smiled. "You are clutch!" he said. "Clutch!"

He ran towards the locker room with the rest of the team and the assistants. He let out a loud "Woo!" before he left the floor.

Al and I were the only two left on the floor from our team. He was a little used player for us who was pressed into action that night because of foul trouble.

I gave him a pat on the head.

"I didn't think you were gonna pass it," Al said.

I wiped the sweat from my forehead and it was no use because my jersey was already drenched.

"Why?" I said.

"Cause I saw this look in your eye," he said. "You looked like you were taking on the whole gym. You looked like you had the world on your shoulders."

"I saw your hands," I said. "You showed me your hands."

After one last high five, he ran into the locker room.

I stayed out on the floor for another ten minutes or so. I wanted to soak that feeling up because I knew there were some unpleasant feelings on the way soon. The gym had cleared out completely except for the janitors who were starting to sweep up.

My body was spent and I just stood there at half-court, feet glued to the floor.

One of the janitors pushed the broom up to my feet and stopped.

"You just finished doing your job, son," he said, with a gap-toothed smile. "Now why don't you let me do mine?"

"Sorry," I said.

"That was clutch, son," he said, as he started

pushing his broom up the floor. Hearing him call me son reminded me of Terrell for a moment, and a chill ran down my spine.

I slowly made my way off the court. My feet burned and my right arm felt raw to the touch. I let out a long sigh. It felt good to get the world off of my shoulders for one night.

FOURTEEN

When I got home from Watts High it was around midnight. My grandmother was asleep in her chair. The TV was on, as usual. I turned it off and went over to her. She was fast asleep and looked peaceful. I didn't want to wake her, even though her bed was more comfortable than that old chair. I covered her with a blanket and turned the lights out in the living room.

———

I was dog tired when my head hit the pillow, but I stopped myself from sleeping. With all that had been going on in the past few weeks, I needed to find some peace. And that meant choosing a college. I peeled myself out of bed and sat down at my desk with two sheets of paper and a pen.

There were two colleges on my final list. Each one got its own sheet. I wrote a plus and minus at the top of both sheets.

Education was the first thing. Like I said to David at his mansion, I wasn't going to be a one—and-done player. I averaged a 3.5 GPA during my time at Inglewood High and it was legitimate. No special treatment for being a star athlete. The college I chose would be my home for four years no matter how basketball turned out for me. The NBA could wait. I planned to take real classes and earn real grades, just like high school. I thought about possible majors and came to the conclusion that I'd study English. I couldn't wait to take classes with students who enjoyed reading books and talking about them as much as I did.

Then I shifted my attention to the geographic location of each school. One of them was at home in LA. I didn't have to think about that too long. The other one was all the way on the East Coast. Could I really be that far away from home? Would I miss my grandmother too much?

Finally, I thought about the colleges in terms of their basketball programs. They were both winning programs in competitive conferences. One of the schools was a traditional powerhouse and the other was a program that had started to dominate more recently. Their levels of TV exposure were neck and neck and both had their healthy share of players who went on to the NBA. The last piece of information to think about was the coaching situation at each of the schools. Making the right choice here would be huge given what I had gone through with Coach. My trust level with coaches—and really, everybody other than my grandmother and Robin—was at an all-time low.

Of the schools on my list, the two coaches couldn't have been any more different from one another. One of them was loud and emotional, just like Coach DeStefano. That caused me to put a minus in the *Coaching* column for that school, but after digging deeper into my memory, the coach in question had left an overall good impression on me during a meeting with him. The second coach was the calm type—more X's-and-O's driven. He was the kind of coach that could talk basketball for hours. When I sat down with him at summer camp, he came prepared and shared with me a detailed look into how I'd fit into their schemes, both offensively and defensively. The last thing up for comparison was the age of each coach. The loud one was older. The calm one was younger.

After all that, I was spent. I looked at my alarm clock and it read three a.m. I could rest easy now. All of the hard work was finally done: I did my job on the court, in the classroom, and at home.

It was time to sleep on it and dream on it.

I closed my eyes and went out like a light.

———

I woke up the next morning and it hit me. I knew where I wanted to go to college.

The deciding factor?

I decided against the school with the coach that reminded me of coach.

———

"You're sure about this, Paul?" my grandmother said at the breakfast table that morning.

I nodded and took a bite of her famous banana-walnut pancakes.

"Okay," she said. "I'm happy for you."

"Thanks, Grandma."

"You going to college is important," she said. "It's important to your parents and your sister."

"I know."

"They would be so proud of you. The kind of man you've become. How you go to class every day. How you take care of me."

"You take care of me," I said. "And the little I do to help out around here is all in return for raising me."

"It helps, Paul," she said. "It all helps."

"How about you, Grandma?"

"What about me?" she said. "Boy, I'll be just fine without you. You need to go on out there and spread your wings. Don't you be worryin' about nothing back here."

"I don't mean that, Grandma," I said. "I want to know what you think of me? I mean, you're the one who has been around me the most. Taught me right from wrong. Supported me. My parents and my sister hardly got a chance to know me. What kind of man do you think I am?"

She chuckled a bit before a cough caught in her throat.

"Where is this coming from, boy?" she said. "I just told you. You're a fine person and you'll get everything that you deserve in life. The first thing being college."

I didn't say anything.

"And, after that, it's all a bonus," she said with a smile.

There was one more person who needed to hear the news.

I would tell him first thing Monday morning.

I knew it was going to be a challenge, my biggest one yet. But I had to do it. My choice felt right. All the other stuff didn't. The list that Coach gave me didn't feel right. Riding in Terrell's car didn't feel right. The party up in the Hills didn't feel right.

Riding the bus felt right.

Going to class felt right.

Being able to look my teammates in the eye felt right.

FIFTEEN

I peeked my head into Coach's office fifteen minutes before first bell on Monday morning.

"Hey Coach, you got a minute?"

"Sure, Paul," he said. "Take a seat."

I sat down in front of him.

"I made my decision."

He sat up in his chair. A smile curled onto his face. "Well."

"I'm going to attend the University of Oregon," I said.

The smile left his face. He didn't say anything at first. He just stared at me for a few seconds.

"Close the door."

I closed it and sat back down.

"I need you to pick one of those schools on my list, Paul," he said with no emotion in his voice. "It doesn't matter which one."

"I'm tired of this shit." I said. "What's in it for you?"

"You really want to know?" he said. "Because if you do, I'll tell you. But it's ugly. All of it."

"I want to know."

"When the scouts figured out that they couldn't get to you with money or cars or fixing the roof on your grandmother's house or whatever, they started to work on me," he said. "That's how it goes."

"Okay," I said. "What are you getting out of it?"

"If I get you to go to any one of those schools on that list, I get a big payout," he said. "Cash in hand, Paul."

I shook my head.

"I shouldn't get something out of this?" he said.

I didn't have anything to say to him anymore.

"These schools will get what they want, Paul," he said. "One way or another."

"Not with me," I said. "Not with me, they won't."

He threw his glasses off and rubbed the bridge of his nose.

"I'm sorry. I made my choice. And I'm sticking with it," I said, before standing up. I turned around to leave.

"Sit down!" he yelled. "Sit your ass down in that chair!"

I turned around and eyed him. Instead of sitting down, I just stood by the door. That was the best he was going to get from me.

"See this is where it gets ugly," he said.

"You don't think it's been ugly?" I shouted. "What more can you throw at me? What other threats do you have?"

"I know you were at the party with Terrell." he said. "I know you talked to an agent there. I know you were the one who found Terrell. I know you left before the cops arrived. I know it all."

"I was there," I said, "but I said nothing to that agent."

"And Terrell?"

"What?" I said. "You know better than I do that Terrell always did what he wanted to do."

"It's a crime," he said.

I shook my head again.

"You lied," he said. "And the NCAA won't look kindly on it."

"You're bluffing," I said.

"Oh? The college you choose isn't gonna want anything to do with you if they hear that you were at a party in the Hollywood Hills with agents crawling around, where one of your teammates overdosed on heroin. Not with your past. Not with what was swirling around you last year."

I felt my eyes start to water even though I tried my damnedest not to let them. I wiped them quickly. Those rumors hurt me. Coach knew that. He knew bringing them up again would cut me to the bone.

"I'll go you even one further," he continued. "Who do you think spread that rumor about you at the party during your campus visit last year? I was paid fifteen thousand dollars to spread that rumor."

"No," I said, shaking my head as a tear rolling down my face. "No. You told me that you would get rid of the rumor and you did."

"How do you think I got rid of it so fast? So easily?" he said. "I came up with it!"

"No."

"You were all set to commit after the visit," he said. "Remember? But a rival school came in at the last minute, came to me and asked if there was any way I could get you to de-commit."

The room got hot and my legs started to wobble. I felt like the walls were going to cave in on me. I crashed down in the chair in front of his desk.

"I made up that rumor, Paul," he said. "And I'll do it again if I have to."

"You'd do that?" I said weakly, unable to catch my breath. "You'd do that to me?"

"I'm telling you I will," he said with a shrug of the shoulders. As serious as a heart attack.

I looked down to the floor and my eyes filled with liquid. They burned so bad that I thought I'd go blind. I looked back up at him and all I saw was a blurry outline. I wiped the tears out of my eyes and he came into focus.

"It's this way or no way, Paul," he said. "It's gotta be this way."

———

Coach owned me.

I sat in front of my locker, quietly after the last bell. I was dressed in my school clothes with no intention of changing into my basketball gear. We had practice and the rest of the guys were starting to pile in. It wasn't until I looked on the whiteboard next to the door and read that our game the following evening was against the team that knocked us out of the playoffs the year before—preventing us from going to ARCO. With all that had happened, I lost track. This was supposed to be the biggest game of the season. But it didn't feel that way to me. The season that started with optimism and a simple goal was now a complicated mess.

I didn't know what to do. I was all out of ideas.

I looked around the locker room at the faces of the other guys. I saw a collection of calm faces. The guys didn't know what was going on between Coach and me. If they did, their faces wouldn't have been calm. They would've looked more like mine.

It hit me, sitting there in the locker room with my teammates. There was only one way I could get what I wanted. I wasn't sure if I could pull it off. But it seemed like the only way.

I couldn't practice. My heart wasn't in it. I wasn't sure if I wanted to be a part of this anymore. Sports were supposed to be pure. But this was far from pure.

I grabbed my backpack and stormed into Coach's office.

"I'm not practicing today," I said.

He looked up at me from his desk. "What about tomorrow?" he said. "Don't you want to play in *that* game, against *them*?"

"I'll let you know tomorrow after school if I'm playing in the game or not," I said. "I can't practice today. If I choose to play, I can do it without practicing. I think I've earned that."

He nodded. "Tomorrow, after school then."

I turned to leave.

"Oh, and Paul," he said to my back.

I turned to look at him.

"Make sure you come in here tomorrow with a decision on college," he said. "A real decision. We need to put an end to all this."

I nodded and left, walked to the locker room, and stopped right before I entered it. I listened to the guys joking and laughing with each other as they got ready for practice. They sounded happy.

Basketball wasn't life and death for them like it seemed to be for me. If I decided to go through with my plan, it would shatter all that for them. All that happiness.

I took the side exit out of school and thought on it during my bus rides home to Watts.

SIXTEEN

It was the morning of the big game.

I got to school bright and early—long before any of the teachers or administrators even—because I wanted to get a full workout in before classes began. I had a key to the locker room that Coach had given to me in case I ever wanted to use the gym off hours.

The workout was the most intense one I had ever gone through in my life. And I was all alone.

I went through all of my drills at full speed: footwork, dribbling, shooting. I ignored the pain and welcomed the burn. The workout ended with fifty sprints up and down the length of the court.

I left pools of my sweat around different spots on the floor. I wiped the spots with some towels from the janitor's closet. After that, I looked around the gym. I saw the empty stands that in twelve hours or so would be filled to the rafters with screaming fans. The biggest game of the year and I wasn't sure if I would step on that floor ever again. A drop of sweat fell onto the floor from my forehead and I bent down with a towel to wipe it dry. While I was down there, I touched the floor with both hands. I stood up and walked to the locker room. I was content if that was the last time I ever sweat on that floor.

I showered up and then headed over to Coach's office.

It was time to stand tall.

I was prepared for anything. I was ready for him to throw me off the team in reaction to what I was about to do. I was also ready to play in the game if things went my way and lead my team to victory against the team that knocked us out of the playoffs the previous year.

All of life's possibilities were open to me at that moment.

I was ready to live life on my terms.

"Paul," Coach said from behind his desk. "What are you doing here this early? I thought you'd be in after final bell."

"I'm ready now," I said. "I thought I'd catch you early."

"Take a seat," he said.

I took a seat.

He eyed me for a moment. His eyes looked tired behind his glasses.

"I looked at everything. Thought about all you had to say," I said. "And I've decided that I'm sticking with my decision."

"You really should reconsider, Paul," he said. "It doesn't have to go this way. You get to go to college and play ball. I get what I want. What are you trying to prove with this?"

"That's not all," I said. "After school, I'm going to walk into the locker room and I'm going to tell the guys everything. About me. Terrell. You. Everything."

He wasn't expecting that. His face twisted with confusion.

"And I'm going to ask the guys if they'll boycott the game with me."

"What?" he said.

"I'm not going to play for you anymore," I said. "And I'm going to ask the guys to do the same."

He was speechless.

"It might not work. I know it probably won't work," I said. "But I'm going to try. It's all I have left."

"Paul," he said. It was all he could say.

"The only way I'll play in the game tonight," I said. "And I mean, the *only* way, is if you are not the coach."

I left the office and had a great day at school.

"Are you okay?" Robin said, as we walked through the halls right after the last bell.

"I'm fine," I said. "How are the pit bulls of South Central doing?"

"It's always a struggle," she said. "They're resilient, though. You know?"

"Yeah," I said.

We reached the gym and stopped at the door. The janitors were inside, sweeping in between the bleachers.

"You'd never come in there," I said, jabbing a thumb toward the door. "Would you?"

She shook her head and then smiled. "Nah, Showtime. That's you."

"Things might be changing around here," I said. "Tonight might be the last of something."

"Things are changing?" she said.

There was a silence and it felt good. I wanted to live in that silence with her. I needed Robin in my life. I needed to trust someone other than my grandmother. I was finally ready for it.

"You think you could find it in your heart to give Showtime a chance?" I said.

"A chance at what?"

"A chance to be your boyfriend?"

She lunged forward and wrapped both her arms around my neck. I picked her up and squeezed her tight. When I put her down, she gave me a kiss right on the lips. She opened her mouth and so did I, letting a little tongue in. But not too much.

"Well, I'm gonna go in there," I said.

"Right," she said. "Don't you have to visualize your great victory and the contributions that you plan on making to that victory?"

"Something like that," I said.

Robin leaned in again and gave me a quick kiss—just a peck. It felt damn good.

"I'm gonna go home and do my science homework," she said. "Never forget about the science homework, Showtime."

And with that, Robin, my girlfriend, walked back down the hall. When she got to the exit at the other end, she turned around, smiled, and gave me a little wave.

I waved back and entered the gym.

———

Two hours before the game, I gathered the team in the locker room. I had my jersey on even though the rest of the guys were in sweats. Coach wasn't there. He was in his office with the door closed. I told the guys everything. Just as I said I would. They listened closely because they looked up to me. Not because I was any kind of authority figure, but because of my skill on the court.

When I asked them whether or not they'd join me in my boycott, there were indecisive looks all around the locker room. And I didn't blame them. If I was in their shoes, I'm not so sure that I would've gone through with it.

I only asked them once. I didn't persist and didn't bully them. After five minutes, Deonte said he'd join me. I took my jersey off and threw it on the floor. Deonte walked over and stood next to me. He peeled his jersey off and tossed it on the floor next to mine. There were two jerseys on the floor, ten more to go. We couldn't go through with it if it wasn't the whole team. It had to be unanimous.

A couple of the other guys walked over and followed suit. The pile of jerseys on the floor grew. After only ten short minutes, the whole team was jersey-less and the pile on the floor was a small mountain.

I walked to Coach's office and knocked on the door.

He opened it and looked at me like I was crazy. "Where's your jersey?" he said.

I nodded my head for him to follow me. He did. We walked into the locker room and he saw the whole team standing there with their jerseys off. He looked to floor and saw the pile. I walked over to my teammates. We stood there, side by side, looking at coach.

He put his head down and walked back into his office and closed the door. Fifteen minutes later, his door opened. He didn't walk back through the locker room. He left the school through the back exit instead.

———

There was ten minutes to go before game time. The rest of the team was out on the floor warming up. I told the guys that I would pass on warming up, because I wanted to preserve my sprained ankle. But that wasn't the truth. I stayed behind because I wanted to savor it. I still had a little time to go before the show. I wasn't sure if this would be my last game or not. If Coach was going to carry out any of his threats or not.

I didn't know what the future held for me.

But I wasn't scared.

There was a calm inside of me that I had never felt before.

I sat there in front of my locker with my eyes closed. The muffled sound of the crowd from the gym was starting to come through. The anticipation had gripped them as well and they were ready to explode. I could tell the gym was filled to capacity too. It's just something that you know, a feeling that you get.

I stood up from my locker and my legs felt sturdy, my feet set firmly on solid ground.

As I walked out of the locker room and down the hallway towards the gym, the sound of the crowd got closer and closer. I could hear them chanting and screaming, waiting for me to step out on that floor.

I thought of my folks and my sister. What would they have thought about my choices? Would they have approved? And what kind of man would they think I've become?

I then thought of my grandmother and felt thankful for her existence. Even at my most lonely and dreadful moments, I could always come home, no matter the hour, and see her sitting in her chair, waiting up for me.

I reached the door to the gym and could feel the bleachers shaking over top of my head. It was time to leave all the serenity behind and toss myself into the frenzied chaos.

I grabbed the handle of the door and smiled. As I walked across the threshold, I thought about pit bulls and science homework, and I proved to myself that I had made it, I had control of my destiny, and most importantly, you can be awake and dream.